A FATAL DECEPTION

P.F. FORD

Editing by KT Editing Services

To my amazing wife, Mary – sometimes we need someone else to believe in us before we really believe in ourselves. None of this would have happened without her unfailing belief and support.

CHAPTER ONE

'I think you've done enough assessing, don't you?' asked Slater. 'Can I go back to work now?'

Sitting in the easy chair opposite, Dr Andrea Newsome looked impassively at Slater through the large round lenses of her spectacles. 'Are you sure you're ready? I have to be sure there are no aftereffects and you're going to be able to cope.'

Slater heaved a frustrated sigh. He wished he'd never heard of Diana Randall. This was all her fault. If she hadn't jumped off that bloody roof, he would never have been undergoing this stupid assessment. 'This is ridiculous,' he snapped. 'You know I'm not crazy, and I certainly don't need a shrink.'

'We've been through this before. No one is suggesting you're crazy, and I'm not a shrink. I'm here to assess you, not declare you insane.'

'I don't need assessing. I just need to get back to work.'

'You make it sound as if I'm going to have you strapped into a straitjacket and carted off for a lobotomy! My job is simply to determine if you're ready to go back to work. It's only been four weeks, and I told you before, we have to go through a process called "watchful waiting".'

'And what exactly are you watchfully waiting for?'

'Signs,' she said. 'Signs that will tell me you have been affected by what happened and need help before you can go back to work, or signs that tell me you are ready to go back to work without any further help.'

'But I am ready,' said Slater.

'So you keep saying, but that's for me to decide.'

He threw his hands up in irritation. 'But I keep telling you, there's nothing wrong with me.'

'Suffering the sort of traumatic shock you endured isn't something to be ashamed of. Diana slipped through your arms and fell off a roof. Of course you feel guilty. Anyone would.'

'She didn't "slip through my arms". I had hold of her, but she conned me into letting go.'

'I'm sorry, I didn't mean to suggest–'

'I had enough trouble convincing Professional Standards I hadn't colluded with her,' he said bitterly. 'I don't need you to start dragging that all up again. She kissed me! It's not exactly the sort of thing you expect a murder suspect to do, and I was so surprised I relaxed my grip. That's when she jumped. She knew exactly what she was doing.'

'I'm sorry, it must have been awful.'

'Of course it was awful, but what was worse was being accused of letting her jump. But you already know all this. We've been through it before, and I'm not doing it again. You'll just have to accept my word. I'm over it.'

Dr Newsome glanced down at her notes. 'But what about the stuff you told me that went with it? Didn't you tell me you couldn't sleep? And what about your appetite? According to my notes, you're not eating properly. It also says here you have no energy. Shall I go on?'

'That was when I first came here and it had just happened. I was exhausted, and a bit shell-shocked.'

'And what about now? Are you still shell-shocked?'

Slater sighed. 'I suppose I am a bit, yes, but I don't see why it's such a big deal. It's because I have nothing to do. I'm bored out of my mind.'

'What about your girlfriend? You've not really told me what's happened to her.'

Slater looked down at the ground. 'I don't have a girlfriend. She was getting itchy feet before I started this job, and then, once I was away for a few nights, it became obvious it was never going to work. She wanted her cake, and she wanted to eat it.'

'So you chose the job over her?'

'If you want to put it like that. I want a partner, I don't want to be involved with someone who just wants to keep me in a cage and manipulate me. Anyway, what's she got to do with anything?'

Dr Newsome put down her pen and looked at him levelly. 'Do you have a problem with women?'

Slater gawped at her. 'What? Why do you ask that?'

'I'm just curious to understand why you've never settled down.'

'Is that really relevant to me going back to work? Or are you just being nosey?'

She bobbed her head to acknowledge his point.

'You show me a happily married copper,' he continued, 'and I'll show you dozens who have been divorced at least once. It goes with the job. It seems to me that if you don't get married, you won't have to go through the hassle of a divorce.'

She looked at him for a long moment, and Slater dropped his eyes to the floor again.

'Tell me how you feel about Jenny now.'

'I don't actually seem to feel anything,' he said.

'Aren't you worried about where she is?'

'Not particularly. She's an adult and she's made her choice. No one asked her to go.'

'Are you saying you don't care about her at all? But wasn't she living with you?'

'Yes, but she was just using me, that's all.' Slater shifted uncomfortably in his chair under the scrutiny of the psychologist, who he knew was studying him carefully. He was struggling to put his feelings into words. In fact, he was struggling to find any feelings towards his former girlfriend, and he was experiencing the uncomfortable realisation that maybe he just didn't have any feelings for anything right now. But then if he said as much, would it condemn him to even more weeks of inactivity?

'You don't seem to know what to say,' she said. 'I want to help you, but I can't put words into your mouth.'

'I can form my own words, thank you,' he muttered.

'But you don't seem to be able to.'

'Maybe I just don't feel anything,' he blurted out.

'And that's normal for you, is it? I understood one of your qualities was empathy. You can't have empathy if you don't have feelings.'

Slater looked down at his hands. He realised he was picking at his fingernails.

'You've been doing that ever since you sat down,' Dr Newsome said. 'Is this something new? Or am I making you nervous today?'

He ignored the question and turned his attention to her legs for a few seconds. He had spent a lot of time studying her legs during these sessions, so he already knew they were very long – and very shapely – but it didn't hurt to be reminded once again.

'I just don't seem to be able to get past it. I need my job to focus upon,' he said eventually, looking up at her. 'It's like my brain's going to waste, and I can't sleep, because every time I close my eyes I just see Diana falling away from me.'

'It's called post-traumatic stress disorder,' Dr Newsome said. 'It's not unusual after such an incident. It's much better to face up to it and deal with it rather than trying to ignore it.'

'Ignore it?' Slater gave a hollow laugh. 'Believe me, I'd give my right arm to ignore it. The problem is, right now I have nothing else to think about. That's why I need to get back to work. Thinking about a case will drive all thoughts of Diana away.'

'But you can't go back to work until I'm convinced you're coping.'

'So what now? Are we just going to go round in circles?'

Dr Newsome smiled. 'Sometimes that's how these sessions work. We ride the merry-go-round until I'm sure you're ready to step off.'

Slater sighed again. 'Yes, I think I understand the concept. I'm just not convinced.'

'Not convinced about what?'

He picked at his fingernails again.

'Not convinced I can help you? Or not convinced you _want_ to be helped?' Dr Newsome asked.

Slater tried to stifle a yawn but couldn't. 'These damned pills you prescribed do nothing but make me sleep. I can't see how they help.'

'I thought you just said you couldn't sleep,' she said. 'It sounds to me as if you're not actually taking the pills as prescribed.'

Slater looked guiltily back down at his hands.

'They won't help if you don't take them.'

'But they turn me into a zombie. I can't drive in that state.'

'You're not supposed to be driving if you're taking them!'

'Exactly,' said Slater. 'How else can I get around? Have you tried catching a bus lately?'

'I thought you had your friend staying with you?' Dr Newsome asked.

'Well, yeah, he is, but he's not there just to drive me around all the time. He's still got his own life to live.'

'But the tablets are there to help you sleep. We all need sleep, even you.' Dr Newsome sat back in her chair and crossed her legs. 'I can't work with you if you won't work with me.'

'I just want to get on with my life and get back to work.'

'And that is our shared dilemma,' she told him. 'Because, believe it or not, that's what I want too. The thing is, I'm the one with the power to say if it's going to happen or not. And let me be honest – do you think I'm likely to give you the all-clear if you won't cooperate?'

'Aww, come on, Andrea, I'm going mad here!'

Her lips twitched for just a moment. 'It's Dr Newsome, as you well know,' she said. 'It would be unethical and unprofessional for me to encourage a familiar relationship with one of my clients.'

Slater grinned. 'How about if I promise to take the sleeping pills every night? Will you let me go back to work then?'

'And how will I know you're taking them?' she asked. 'And before you ask, no, I will not come to your room every night to make sure.'

Slater blushed guiltily. Was he really so transparent?

'Yes, you can be quite transparent,' she said, as if she had read his mind. 'Perhaps if you didn't stare at my legs all the time. . .'

Slater squirmed under her gaze and the silence seemed to stretch out for hours.

'We haven't spoken about DS Brearley much, have we?' Dr
Newsome asked suddenly. 'How do you get on with her?'

Slater shrugged. 'She's very competent.'

'That's rather noncommittal. She speaks very highly of you. She
was very quick to speak in your defence. Very loyal.'

Slater felt a touch guilty. 'I've not worked with her for long,' he
said, 'but I believe she's probably as good a DS as I'm ever likely to
work with.'

'That's high praise indeed,' Dr Newsome said. 'So she has made an
impression. Do you enjoy being with her?'

'I enjoy working with her. If you're trying to suggest there's
anything else going on, you're wrong.'

'Would you like there to be something else going on? After all, she
is very attractive. I can't believe you haven't noticed.'

Slater couldn't prevent the wry smile that accompanied his next
line. 'It would be unethical and unprofessional for me to encourage a
familiar relationship . . .'

She smiled. 'I'm sorry. My professional curiosity is getting the
better of me. I don't mean to pry.'

'That's okay. You can pry as much as you want, there's nothing to
find there.'

She studied his face for a moment, then she seemed to make a decision. 'Okay, here's the deal,' she said with a reassuring smile. 'I'll admit
the pills you currently take deliver a pretty hefty dose, but I am
prepared to give you a new, weaker prescription if you promise you will
take them every night. They will help you sleep, but they won't knock
you for six.

'I also insist you add my phone number to your mobile phone
before you leave here, because your second promise is to ring me once
a week to let me know how you're doing, and call me at any time if you
feel you're not coping. That's any time, night or day, I want to know,
right?'

Slater couldn't quite believe his ears. He had been convinced she
was going to say no. 'Really? I can go back to work?'

'If you agree to my conditions and keep those two promises.'

'Of course I will! I'll even get my DS to make sure I take the tablets every night.'

'I mean it about the phone calls. Don't just pay lip service to it. If you do have a problem, I won't be able to help you if you keep it to yourself. If I send you back and it goes pear-shaped, you'll be back on assessment for months, and there won't be a thing I can do to stop it.'

'What happens now?' asked Slater. 'How soon can I start?'

'I will speak to your boss this afternoon and send him my report. The final decision is his, but he's never argued with one of my assessments before. As for how soon, that's up to him, but I'm sure he won't keep you waiting long.'

CHAPTER TWO

Norman Norman had been friends with Slater for more than three years. They had hit it off more or less from the day they started working together, and now he regarded Slater as his best friend.

When he had heard Slater needed help after the traumatic conclusion of his last case, he had immediately volunteered to move into his spare room, and that's how he came to be living there now.

He had just parked his car and puffed his way to the front door, laden with shopping. As he opened the door, he could hear the telephone ringing. He rushed through the door, slamming it shut behind him, dropped the bags of shopping on the floor, and grabbed the phone. 'Hello?'

He listened as the caller made his introduction. It was Bradshaw, Dave Slater's boss.

'You've got some front, calling here,' said Norman.

'What's that supposed to mean?'

'I suppose you want to speak to Dave? Well, tough, he's not here.'

'I know he's not there,' Bradshaw said. 'I'm rather hoping he's attending his assessment appointment right now. That's why I'm calling. It's you I want to speak to. I need your help.'

'What about the investigation? You're hanging Dave out to dry, and you want me to help you? What kind of a friend do you think I am?' Norman said angrily.

'It rather sounds as though you're a misinformed one,' replied Bradshaw calmly. 'I'm not sure where you get your information, but I'm afraid you seem to have the wrong end of the stick. A suspect dies, Professional Standards investigate. You should have been around long enough to know how this works.'

'Now you're talking in riddles,' said Norman. 'I'm talking about the disciplinary investigation.'

'The riddles seem to be coming from your direction. There is no disciplinary investigation.'

Norman was quiet for a moment. 'I'm not with you. I was told Dave was going to be the subject of a disciplinary--'

'Oh, I see. And I suppose you got this news from . . .'

'I'm not revealing my sources,' said Norman hastily. 'I'm not going to give you an excuse to pick on someone else.'

'Now just a minute,' Bradshaw said. 'You really have got the wrong end of the stick. I'm not picking on anybody. You should know me well enough from the old days to know I'm not like that. I never have been, and I never will be. Detective Inspector Slater is not, I repeat, <u>not</u>, under investigation. Detective Sergeant Brearley is also not under investigation, and she will not <u>be</u> under investigation, even if she is the person who has wrongly informed you.'

'What about this rumour I've heard?'

'That's all it was. Someone, somewhere heard Detective Inspector Styles complaining because they had lost a murderer. That someone then decided to blow things out of all proportion, and before you know it, there's a rumour doing the rounds. I've spoken to Styles myself and he has assured me that although he was very angry at the time because they had a sure-fire conviction, he doesn't blame Slater for what happened, and he has no intention of making any formal complaint.'

'Are you sure about this?'

'Of course I am, and I'm disappointed you feel the need to doubt me.'

Norman felt somewhat uncomfortable as he thought about this.

He had worked with Bradshaw many years ago, and it was true the man had a reputation for looking after his officers. Maybe they had all been a bit too quick to judge him and jump to Dave's defence.

'I've known Dave for a few years now,' Norman said, more reasonably now. 'He's more than just an old colleague. He's probably the best friend I've ever had, so I'm always ready to cover his back if there's shit heading his way.'

'I understand that,' said Bradshaw, 'which is exactly why I've come to you to ask for your help.'

'What sort of help?'

Bradshaw sighed. 'I understand he got rather attached to Jenny Radstock.'

'You know very well he did, but that relationship ran its course and died a death while he was away. I think he realised she was going to be much too demanding. I believe he may even have told her to clear off.'

'Why do you say that?'

'I get the feeling he was expecting her to have moved out when he got back. He just didn't seem too bothered that she had gone. In fact, he still doesn't seem to care.'

'Have you talked to him about it?'

'It's quite difficult to talk to him about anything, really,' said Norman. 'He's still pretty touchy about having to see a shrink and be assessed. Right now, he seems to think everyone is involved in this assessment, and he tends to view all questions with suspicion.'

'It's just standard procedure after an incident of that nature,' Bradshaw said quickly.

'Hey, you don't need to explain that to me. I'm not the one who doesn't understand it's for his own good. The problem is, all this hanging around is driving him crazy. He just wants to get back to work.'

'Do you think he's ready?'

'It's probably just what he needs, but it's not up to me, is it?'

'I spoke to the psychologist yesterday,' said Bradshaw. 'She says he's as good as ready, so fingers crossed, maybe he'll do enough to convince her this morning.'

'Let's hope so,' said Norman. 'Anyway, what was it you wanted me to do?'

'I want you to find Jenny.'

Norman laughed. 'Are you kidding? If Dave doesn't want her around, he's not going to be too happy if I bring her back, is he?'

'I don't want you to bring her back. I just want to know where she is. Right now, she seems to have gone completely off the radar.'

'Maybe she's gone off the radar because she doesn't want to be found. Have you thought of that?'

'Yes, I have. If that's the case, then so be it, but I want to know for sure, and I think Slater would want to know too, deep down.'

'How come she disappeared anyway?' Norman asked. 'I thought you were watching her.'

'After the first month with Slater, we were quite satisfied she was no longer being watched or followed, so I stood my people down.'

'I see. Was that a mistake?'

'So far, I've no reason to believe it was, but I can't deny that the fact she's disappeared is a concern. The thing is, I couldn't justify spending the money on what was really a favour to her parents.'

'It was never an official protection job?'

'Let's just say I was bending a few rules.'

'Well, I can tell you now, she hasn't left any clues here. I've been all over the place ,and there's absolutely nothing to tell us where she's gone,' said Norman.

'No one just vanishes into thin air. I'm sure she hasn't left the country, so she must be here somewhere.'

'Until we have some sign, I have no idea where to start. You're the guy with the resources. If you can't find her, how the hell can I?' Norman asked.

'The minute she switches her phone on, I shall know,' said Bradshaw.

'You realise she could easily have ditched it. She's probably got her hands on a new one by now.'

'Yes, that thought has crossed my mind, but I'm hoping there's some other reason she's not used it.'

'She's not stupid,' Norman said. 'She knows she can be tracked by that phone. My guess is she's not used it because she doesn't want anyone to find her.'

'Look,' Bradshaw said, sounding weary, 'I know it's a long shot, but it's worth a try.'

'I suppose if you could give me somewhere to start, I might be prepared to try to find her,' said Norman grudgingly. 'But what am I supposed to tell Dave?'

'Let me worry about him.'

'You'll need to get him out of the way somehow or he's going to know what I'm up to, and he'll want to come along and help.'

'He'll get the all-clear to come back to work today, and when he does, I have a job lined up for him that will keep him out of the way for a while.'

'You sound very confident he's going to be passed fit for work,' Norman said thoughtfully.

'Like I said, I spoke to his doctor yesterday . . .'

'Oh, I get it. You've told her to send him back to work, right?'

'You'll help me? That's a definite yes, is it?' asked Bradshaw, ignoring Norman's question.

'I'll think about it, but I need to know how this is gonna work. I mean, I'm not a charity. I need to make a living.'

'You'll be working for me as a special detective. Let's call it a consultant position. I'll send you a contract so it's all above board.'

'Do I get a badge?' Norman asked eagerly. 'It's much easier to ask questions when there's a badge involved. It makes it more official.'

'Yes, you do get a badge, but you won't be a police officer. Anyone who looks closely at the badge will know that, and they won't have to speak to you if they don't want to.'

Norman thought for a moment. 'You know, technically I am still recovering from a heart attack, so I'm going to need some help.'

'Who do you have in mind?'

'I'm assuming you will put Watson with Dave to keep an eye on him and let me know if he starts to get suspicious.'

'Correct,' said Bradshaw. 'If you were hoping for her help, I'm afraid you'll have to manage without her.'

'That's okay. I'd rather she was watching Dave. I have someone else in mind to work with me.'

'Who's that?'

'Her name is Naomi Darling,' said Norman. 'She's just quit the force, but she's good at what she does, and she's a good foil for me.'

'I don't think I know her,' said Bradshaw.

'That's not a problem. I know her, and I trust her. And I know you can trust her.'

There was silence on the line as Bradshaw considered, then finally he spoke.

'Alright, if it means I get your help, that's good enough for me.'

'She'll need a contract too.'

Bradshaw sighed. 'I'll draw up a contract for her too.'

'And you will make sure Dave is out of the way?'.

'Consider it done. I think you'll find Detective Inspector Slater will be much happier when he gets home today.'

'Okay, you come back to me when you've got him out of the way.'

'Is that a yes?'

'It's a probably,' said Norman. 'Get Dave out of the way, get those contracts set up, and give me somewhere to start. Then we might just have a deal.'

———

Detective Sergeant Samantha Brearley, aka Watson, was Slater's partner. She had been educated at a private girl's school and gone on to join the army, where she discovered the joys of detective work in the RMP. After leaving the army, she joined the police force, where her career was nearly ended by a bullet that shattered one of her knees.

However, Watson wasn't one for giving up. She insisted her surgeon replace her shattered knee with a new one, which she told everyone was her 'bionic knee' and would enable her to get back to work. True to her word, she had done exactly that and was as now as fit as anyone.

If asked what he thought of her, Slater would have described her as tall, athletic, and good-looking, in a 'posh bird' sort of way. He also thought she was a great partner to work with: intelligent, thoughtful, and well-organised. If he was feeling particularly honest, he would even admit she was probably the best partner he could possibly have.

She could, however, be rather straight-laced at times, and he enjoyed pointing this out and ribbing her at every opportunity. She took all this in the spirit it was intended and actually enjoyed the banter, which was something she had never encountered before.

She had learnt very quickly that Slater was happy to take it as well as dish it out. She knew that if she bided her time, she would always get an opportunity to get her own back – and she always did. Watson thought working alongside Slater was probably the happiest she had ever been at work.

They had decided over the phone that there was no point in taking two cars and had decided to use Slater's. Watson regarded this as a bonus because he owned a Range Rover and was usually happy to let her drive. How often was a girl likely to get such an opportunity?

'Where to, Watson?' he asked as he bundled her case into the back of the car.

'North,' she said. 'We're off to Northumberland.'

'You realise that's where Norman was sent when he was in exile for three years, don't you? He says it's nothing but open moorland and sheep. And there are no people.'

'I think you'll find that's a slight exaggeration. We've got an old murder to investigate, and you can't have murders without people, can you?'

'You can tell me about it on the way.'

'If you let me drive, you can read about it,' she said. 'That way you can make sure you don't miss any the details.'

Slater grinned. 'You realise it's going to take us hours to drive that far?'

She smiled back at him. 'I certainly do, but you know you get bored driving.'

'But I'm not bored yet. You ride shotgun until we stop for lunch, and we'll swap places after that. Until then, you can read me a story about an old murder case.'

CHAPTER THREE

Although he was staying at Slater's, officially Norman still lived in a room above a pub in town. He made a point of calling in two or three times a week to keep in touch with his landlord and collect any mail.

It would be fair to say Norman didn't get a great deal of mail, and what he did get usually consisted of bills, spam sales letters, and assorted leaflets, so he was surprised to find a letter in a handwritten blue envelope waiting for him. There was something vaguely familiar about the handwriting, and he was sure he should know whose it was, but he couldn't quite place the writer.

He carried the letter and a cup of coffee across to a table in the deserted pub and placed them down next to each other. He frowned and scratched his head as he settled in a chair and carefully tore the blue envelope open. There was a letter inside, written on matching blue paper, and as he unfolded it, he glanced quickly at the signature. He did a double take and let out a low whistle.

'How spooky is that?' he said out loud. 'Wherever you are, Jenny, your ears must be burning right now.'

By the time he had finished reading the letter, he found his right hand had involuntarily moved up to cover his mouth. He gazed out of the window at nothing in particular, trying to make sense of what he had just read. After a minute or so, he shook his head in defeat and returned his attention to the letter again. Maybe this time it would make more sense.

He re-read the letter and then slowly shook his head again. He thought for a moment or two, then reached into his pocket, pulled out his mobile phone, and dialled a number.

'Are you busy right now?' he asked when the familiar voice answered his call.

'Do you mean in general or right this minute?' asked Naomi Darling.

'Let me rephrase that. How soon can you get here?'

'You sound worried. Is there a problem you need help with?'

'I may be speaking out of turn, but I think you mentioned you needed a job,' said Norman. 'It just so happens I've been offered one for myself, but I told my customer I'm going to need some help.'

'I'm on my way,' she said. 'Where are you? At Dave's?'

'No, the pub. I just called in to say hello.'

'Stay there. Don't do anything until I get there.'

————

'Here, read this, and then tell me what you make of it,' said Norman when Darling joined him half an hour later. He handed her the letter and indicated a chair.

She took it and looked at him expectantly. 'What is it?'

'That's a good question,' he said. 'Go ahead and read it, then tell me what you think. I need a second opinion. I'll go and make some coffee so you can read it on your own. I'll be back in a few minutes.'

He wandered across the bar and banged his way through the door into the kitchen. He had lived here long enough to be treated like part of the family, and he often helped out in the pub if he was at a loose end. As he came back into the room carrying the two coffees, Naomi looked up, a puzzled expression on her face.

'What the hell is this all about?'

'You have no idea either?' he said, as he sat down next to her.

'That's a pity. I was hoping it was just some vague woman thing and you would know what she was on about.'

'Actually, it's not that women are vague. The problem is you guys don't listen properly,' she said. 'As for this letter, I'm afraid being a woman is no help. I have no idea what it means.'

'Crap!' said Norman. 'I was hoping that maybe she had told you something previously that might give us a clue.'

'The only person who might have some idea is Dave, but I'm not sure showing him this now would be such a good idea. Personally, I think he's better off without her, whatever the reason for them splitting up.'

'Yeah, well, I can't argue with that.'

'Did this arrive this morning?' Darling asked.

Norman nodded. 'Yeah, it makes a change from the usual bills.'

'She's saying she pissed him off on purpose so they would fall out, and he'd be glad to see the back of her.'

'That's how I understood it,' he said.

'What the heck can she be doing that she doesn't want him to get involved in?' she asked. 'It sounds to me like she's either being very melodramatic or it really is something very dodgy.'

'Yeah, that's what I thought.'

Darling studied Norman's face for a few seconds. 'This isn't the job you were talking about, is it? It's not that I don't want to help you, Norm. You know I'd love to. But I can't afford to be working for nothing looking for some empty-headed drama queen. I need to be earning money.'

Norman raised his eyebrows. 'I didn't realise you disliked her so much.'

'It's not so much that I dislike her. It's more a case of I like Dave, and I've always thought she was using him. I don't like that.'

'But you have to admit the tone of that letter suggests she cares about him,' Norman argued.

'I suppose there's a first time for everything, but I think I'll reserve judgement on her sincerity, if it's all the same to you.'

'You've never said any of this stuff before.'

'You never asked me, and who am I to tell Dave how to live his life? Besides, who's to say I'm right.'

'But would you help me look for her?' asked Norman.

'I already said, I'm not working for nothing,' she said, adamantly.

'I promise you, if you join me on this, you will be earning money,' said Norman.

'Really? How's that going to work? Have you won the lottery?'

'I wouldn't exactly say that. But I have been engaged in a professional capacity, and I insisted you would have to be working alongside me if I was going to do the job.'

Darling peered at him curiously. 'Engaged by whom?'

'Does the name Bradshaw ring a bell?'

It took a few seconds for the name to register. 'Dave's boss?'

'That's the guy.'

'But I thought he was public enemy number one?'

'I think we got that wrong,' Norman confessed. 'Apparently there is no disciplinary, and there never was going to be one. We were misinformed.'

'What about Dave? He's going to want to be in on this, isn't he?'

'He's going to be sent away to work on another job. He won't know anything about what we're doing.'

Naomi took a long, appraising look at him. 'And what about you? How are you feeling now?'

'I'm fine.'

Darling snorted derisively. 'Yeah, right.'

'No, I am, honestly,' Norman said, plastering on a smile.

She gave him a sympathetic smile of her own. 'Remember, you're not the only one here who's been trained to detect bullshit. I can promise you, your eyes and your words don't match.'

Norman sighed. 'Fine. I'm still hurting a bit, but it is what it is. I'll get over it. I've had to deal with worse than this before now.'

'Do you want to talk about it?'

'What is there to say?' he said sadly. 'Once her kids got it into their heads it was my fault their daddy had been sent away, there was only ever going to be one thing I could do. It wouldn't be right to ask Jane to choose between me and her children, would it? If they were adults, it might have been a bit different ball game, but they're just little kids struggling to understand.'

'That must have been hard for all of you,' she said.

'That's an understatement.' Then the false smile appeared again. 'Anyway, I don't want to dwell on that. I'm just trying to look forward. At least now I'm fit enough to start working again, so I reckon if I can keep busy, I'll get over it that much quicker. What do you say to this job? Are you in?'

She patted his arm. 'Hell yeah! Why not? Let's do it. At least then I'll be able to keep an eye on you and make sure you really are okay.'

CHAPTER FOUR

Norman adjusted the phone between his ear and shoulder. 'You already knew where she was, didn't you?'

'I've had an alert out ever since she disappeared,' Bradshaw said. 'There have been one or two possible sightings, but nothing definite until just after I called you.'

'We've got somewhere to start now. That's good. Where is it? North, south, or what?'

'Oh, I can do better than that. I can tell you exactly where she is. It's a town called Redville-on-Sea, down on the south coast. I can even give you the exact address where you can find her.'

Norman felt his enthusiasm rapidly draining away. He had seen this job as a chance to get back into the swing of investigating, but if Bradshaw already knew where she was . . . 'I suppose this is a courtesy call to tell me the job's off?'

'On the contrary! The job is very much on,' said Bradshaw decisively.

'But if you know where she is, what do you need me for?'

'Because it looks as if she's lying on a mortuary slab, waiting for someone to identify her.'

Norman experienced a sharp, involuntary intake of breath. It had never occurred to him that Jenny might be dead. 'Holy shit! Are you sure it's her?'

'A body was found in a derelict squat two weeks ago. It's been reported as a suicide. It was only brought to my attention because she seems to be about the right age, and she has the same natural hair colour. I've been sent photos, but her hair's been dyed so I really can't be sure. It needs someone who knows her to confirm her identity.'

'You know her. Surely you could do that yourself.'

'Yes, I could, but you know her better, and you've seen her more recently.'

'Does Dave know about this?' Norman asked.

'We don't even know for sure that it's her. I think she needs to be formally identified before we start telling anyone anything.'

Norman was dubious. 'Do you think keeping him in the dark is the right way to play this?'

'Honestly? I don't know, but I wouldn't want to risk having a vengeful Dave Slater on the loose. Much better if it's a fait accompli when he finds out. And don't forget that he's only just got over the Diana Randall death. I don't think it's a good idea to tell him about this right now.'

Norman sighed. 'I hope you know what you're doing.'

'It's like walking a tightrope,' admitted Bradshaw, 'and I know I could easily be getting it all wrong and end up falling off. If I _am_ wrong, I'll just have to deal with the fallout. What about you? If you'd rather not get involved, I quite understand.'

'I already am involved now I know she's dead. What exactly do you want me to do?'

'At the moment, I need you to identify her and then find out what happened to her.'

'You don't think it's a suicide, then?'

'I don't know, Norm. It just doesn't sit right with me, but that may be because I don't want to believe it. I need someone I can trust to remain impartial. That's why I've come to you. Will you do this for me?'

Norman had been on the verge of telling Bradshaw about the letter he had received from Jenny, but instinct told him he should keep that to himself. Norman always listened to his instincts.

'Sure, Naomi and I can do it,' said Norman, 'but don't think I'm doing it just for you. I knew Jenny, and I'd like to find out what happened to her.'

'Thank you, Norm,' said Bradshaw. 'I really appreciate this.'

'So, what happens next?'

'I'll email the contracts to you, the address where the body can be found, and what information I have so far. I'm also going to find out who handled the investigation into her death and arrange for you to speak to them. If you need anything, call me.'

CHAPTER FIVE

'It's a good job you lost all that weight,' observed Darling as Norman slipped into the passenger seat of her car and clicked his seat belt on.

'If you're going to start making jokes about how the seat belt would never have reached all the way round, don't bother. I'm sure I must have heard every one at least dozen times, courtesy of Dave Slater.'

She looked across at him and smiled. 'Actually, I wasn't going to mention seat belts. I was just going to point out how small the interior of my car is before you started complaining about it.'

'Who me? I never complain,' said Norman indignantly.

She rolled her eyes. 'Yeah, right. Of course you don't.'

'Besides,' he said, ignoring her sarcasm, 'I don't need much room. These days, I'm half the man I was.'

'This time I hope that is a reference to your size and nothing else. Although I think half is possibly a bit of an exaggeration, don't you?'

'It's just a figure of speech, as you well know, unless you're being painfully pedantic.' Norman rubbed his much-diminished stomach. 'I happen to be particularly proud of the fact I've taken heed of my doctor's advice and put the work in to improve my health.'

She reached across and patted his knee. 'And you should be proud of what you've done,' she said, as she put the car into gear and eased away. 'I'm proud of you for what you've achieved too!'

Norman beamed with pleasure. 'You are?'

'Of course I am. I know exactly how hard you've had to work. I was there at the start, remember?'

Norman inclined his head in acknowledgement as he recalled how she had indeed been there at the start, nagging and urging him in the beginning, and then cheering him on as it became a bit easier. She had kept it up for two months before she had finally left him to carry on alone. Now he felt he owed it to her to continue to keep himself in shape.

'Yeah, I know,' he said. 'I wonder if I would have kept at it if you hadn't been there.'

'That's irrelevant. I was there, and you did keep at it. That's all that matters.'

'But you didn't have to do it.'

'What's a girl supposed to do? I'd just found myself a surrogate dad, and then he nearly died on me. You didn't really think you were getting away from me that easily? Of course I'm gonna help you recover. I want a few more years out of you yet.'

Norman was beaming so much his face was beginning to ache. Darling tended to have that effect on him. If she wanted him as a surrogate dad, that was fine by him. He was proud to regard her as his surrogate daughter.

They drove in silence for a few minutes until they were clear of town and out on the open road. 'Right then,' she said. 'Where exactly are we headed?'

'It's a place called Redville-on-Sea on the south coast.'

'Never heard of it.'

'Me neither, until Bradshaw told me this morning. Just head for Brighton and we'll set the sat-nav later.'

'You promised you'd tell me about this case once we got going, so what do we know so far?'

'What we have,' Norman said, 'is a Jane Doe lying on a slab waiting to be identified. Bradshaw told me he couldn't be sure it was Jenny from the photos, and quite frankly I can't tell for sure either. I think it's her, but I need to see her in the flesh to be sure.

'Apparently, they haven't been able to find any dental records for her, which I find hard to believe as she had perfect teeth. It was one of the things that made her stand out in a crowd of homeless people. She would be the only one with a gleaming white smile!'

'I assume you have a backup plan if you're not sure it's her?' asked Darling.

'She left a hairbrush at Dave's. I'm assuming they can get enough DNA from that.'

'What else do we know?'

'They're saying she overdosed on heroin.'

Darling raised an eyebrow. 'Was she a user? I didn't know that.'

'You and me both,' Norman said. 'And I can't see it. She was living with Dave for months, and for most of that time they were pretty cosy, if you see what I mean. He surely would have known, and there's no way he would have ignored it. He would have got her help to get cleaned up.'

'Maybe she had started using and that's what they argued about,' Darling suggested. 'Maybe that's why she left. Perhaps he told her to quit or leave.'

Norman didn't say anything for a moment, and she took her eyes off the road long enough to glance across at him. 'Norm? Are you okay?'

He looked across at her. 'Yeah, I'm fine. I just can't believe I hadn't thought of that myself. I guess that just to goes to show the value of working with a partner. Two heads are better than one, huh?'

'It's just a suggestion. I could be way off the mark.'

'But you could also be right on the mark.'

'He would have told you, wouldn't he?' Darling asked.

Norman was silent for a moment. 'I think he would, but I couldn't say for sure. He seems to have had a lot to deal with over the past year or so, and it's made him a bit more reticent. I'm not sure he would have admitted they'd fallen out if it wasn't so glaringly obvious she's not there any more.'

'You've had a lot to deal with yourself. You nearly died, for God's sake, but it hasn't changed you.'

'Yeah, maybe, but we're not all the same, are we?' Norman smiled fondly at her. 'And don't forget, that's one of the things he's had to deal with. He still feels it was his fault I had that heart attack.'

'Yes, well, he's probably right.' Darling tightened her grip on the wheel. 'If he hadn't been acting like an idiot, you wouldn't have been wrestling with him, and--'

'Yeah, you can blame him if you want, but you're missing the point,' Norman said quickly. 'It wasn't his fault I was in such poor shape, was it? In fact, I should have listened to him a bit more. He was always telling me about all the crap I was eating and how I should lose some weight. I was an accident waiting to happen, and I was fortunate it happened when there were two people there to look after me.'

Darling turned to look at him again.

'What?' he said. 'It could have happened when I was at home on my own. D'you think we'd be sitting here talking like this if it had?'

'Don't talk like that,' she said, turning back to the road.

'I'm just saying it how it is. Dave saved my life.'

It was quite clear this particular conversational thread was over, and Darling didn't say anything for a minute or two. Norman decided he'd made his point, but he didn't intend to make a big deal of it.

'Anyway,' he continued, 'according to the report, she took an overdose of heroin.'

Darling was quick to pick up on his tone. 'But you don't think so.'

'They found a syringe sticking out of her left arm.'

'And that's odd because?'

'She was left-handed. Now, I've never tried to inject myself,' said Norman, 'but if I was going to, I think I'd want to use my steadiest hand, wouldn't you?'

'I see what you mean. It's unlikely, isn't it? But then, if you didn't know she was left-handed, why would you think there was anything suspicious about it? Maybe this proves the girl in the photo can't be Jenny because she's right-handed.'

Norman pursed his lips thoughtfully. 'Yeah, maybe.'

'What else do we know about the scene?'

'Not much. I've only seen a few photos taken in the mortuary, but Bradshaw's arranging for us to speak with the officers who found the body and wrote up the report. I'm hoping we're gonna know a lot more after that.'

'Norm, we're not just going to identify a body, are we?'

'How d'you mean?' he asked.

'It doesn't need two of us to identify a body, does it? And we have accommodation booked. What's really going on here?'

Norman puffed out a breath. 'Bradshaw doesn't think it was suicide. He wants us to find out what really happened.'

Darling looked at him intently. 'What about you? Do you think it wasn't suicide?'

'I'm trying to keep an open mind. Jenny never struck me as the suicidal type, and the syringe in the left arm makes me very suspicious.'

'Not such a completely open mind, then?'

'And that's one of the reasons you're here,' said Norman. 'You hardly knew her, so you have no preconceived notion of what she would or wouldn't have done. Add the fact that you don't have a very high opinion of her, and you should be the perfect foil should I fail to keep my perspective. You have a reputation for saying what you think, so I expect you to say if you think I'm wearing blinkers.'

She flashed a wicked grin at him. 'Oh, I will, Norm, don't worry. You can count on that.'

CHAPTER SIX

As the sheet was pulled back, Norman stared at the face that had been revealed. She looked far more peaceful than he could ever recall her looking in life, especially when he remembered how snippy she could be. For a weird moment, he found himself hoping she would suddenly open her eyes and direct some sarcasm his way, just to prove they were all incompetent and she'd been alive all along.

'Yeah, that's her alright,' he said. 'Her name is Jenny Radstock. I see her hair is black again.'

'It's not her natural colour,' said the pathologist.

'Yeah, I know. The black was part of a disguise. In reality, she was fiery by colour, and fiery by nature. She could be as sweet as you like one minute and then slice you into little pieces with just a few words the next.'

'You sound like you knew her well.'

'She was involved in a case I was working on one time,' said Norman. 'And then recently she lived with a friend of mine for a while. We weren't exactly best friends, but I knew her well enough, I guess.'

He nodded to the technician to re-cover her face, and turned to the pathologist. 'You know we're here to look into what happened, right?'

Doctor Morton was a studious man who was approaching retirement – and very much looking forward to it. He shifted uncomfortably from foot to foot. 'It all seems a bit cloak and dagger, if you don't mind me saying. It could put me in a very awkward position with the locals. I have to work with these officers, you know.'

'Let's get something straight before we start,' said Norman. 'We're not Professional Standards or anything like that, and we're not here to make life difficult for anyone. We're not even police officers. We work more on a consultancy basis. We've been called in because Miss Radstock was working in what you might call an undercover situation, and we need to make sure she hadn't been compromised.'

Norman tried to avoid the incredulous look from Darling that he could feel boring into his skull.

'You mean you think she may have been murdered?' asked the pathologist.

Norman gave him a small, conspiratorial smile. 'We need to eliminate that possibility. Of course, the nature of our inquiry means discretion is essential on all sides.'

'Of course,' Dr Morton said hurriedly. 'I understand.'

'Can you run us through your findings?'

'I've prepared a copy for you, and I sent a report to the police.'

'Look, we've literally just arrived,' Norman said. 'The police officer we need to speak to is unavailable until tomorrow. That's why we came straight here. This way, if we have any questions, you can answer them for us. So, if you wouldn't mind?'

Morton sighed. 'It's in my office. Come on through. It will be far more comfortable in there anyway.'

They followed him through to his office and took the two chairs he indicated. 'There isn't that much to tell, really,' he said as he opened a filing cabinet and reached for a file. 'She was found in a dingy squat at the back of Claremont Road. The area is pretty squalid and littered with squats. It's where most of the town's down-and-outs live, so finding a young woman with a syringe hanging from her arm wasn't exactly a surprise.'

He opened the file and began scanning the report. 'Although in her case, there were one or two anomalies.'

'Yeah? Like what?' asked Norman.

'Well, for a start, she wasn't as undernourished as I would have expected. In fact, she seemed remarkably healthy for someone living in that area. I assumed she must have been a recent arrival, and she hadn't been living rough for long.'

'That adds up,' said Norman. 'What else?'

'She wasn't a regular user.'

Norman turned to Darling. 'Didn't I tell you that?'

'I only found three needle marks, so I'd say she had only just started using,' continued Morton. 'And I might be able to suggest why.'

'Go on,' Norman urged.

'She had clearly been involved in some sort of accident, as her right foot was damaged, her right ankle was badly sprained, there was a fracture to her right tibia, and heavy bruising to her right calf and thigh. It's difficult to say with any certainty, but I believe this damage occurred approximately two or three days before she died.'

'Jeez, that would've been painful, wouldn't it?' asked Norman.

'Very,' said Morton. 'Maybe the heroin was meant to take the pain away.'

'That's a bit of a drastic way to kill pain,' Darling said.

'But readily available in the area where she was found,' said Morton. 'And if you're desperate enough . . .'

'Any idea what caused the injuries?' asked Norman.

'Again, it's difficult to say with any certainty.'

'Perhaps it was the trusty blunt instrument?' Darling suggested. 'Do you think she'd had a beating?'

'That's possible,' Morton said, 'but the bruising was also consistent with her having been hit by a car or a vehicle of some sort. Whatever the cause of her injuries, it didn't appear she'd had any sort of treatment for them.'

'Christ,' said Norman. 'She must have been in agony, and there was no one there to help her.'

Morton sighed, shook his head, and returned to the report. 'Although she was well nourished, she hadn't eaten anything recently. Her stomach was virtually empty.'

'What about bloods?' asked Norman.

Morton consulted the report. 'Enough heroin to kill two of her, but nothing else untoward.'

'No booze or anything like that?'

'Not a thing. Apart from the heroin, she was squeaky clean, so to speak.'

'So what's your conclusion?'

'Accidental suicide. I think she was using the heroin to take away the pain, but she used too much.'

'I can see why you might think that,' Norman said, 'but there's something you didn't know that might make you think again.'

Morton looked perplexed.

'She was left-handed.'

'What?'

'She was left-handed,' Norman said again.

Morton looked shocked, but words seemed to fail him.

'Like I said, you didn't know that,' said Norman, 'but now you do, does it make a difference to what you think happened?'

'I just report my findings,' said Morton. 'It's up to the police what they make of them.'

'Yeah, but you're an intelligent man. You must have an opinion, and I'd like to know what it is.'

'In light of what you've just told me, I have to admit it's possible someone else administered the heroin.'

'Wouldn't that be murder then?' Darling said.

'Well, yes, it's a possibility, but at the time I didn't know she was left-handed.'

Darling gave him a sharp look. 'I thought there were ways of determining that from the wear and tear on a person's hands or something.'

'Yes there are, but I was told it was suicide, so I--'

'You really don't want to finish that sentence in front of us,' said Norman, getting to his feet. 'We might not be Professional Standards, but I'd be duty-bound to notify them if you finished saying what I think you were going to say. If I could just have that report you said you had ready for us.'

Morton swallowed hard. He reached for a report on his desk and handed it to Norman.

'C'mon, Naomi,' said Norman. 'Let's get out of here.'

CHAPTER SEVEN

Neither Norman or Darling had been in the best of moods by the time they had left the pathologist's office yesterday afternoon. They were both beginning to think that Jenny's death had been filed as a 'junkie, we've got more important things to worry about' case, which meant no one had tried very hard to look beyond the easy answer.

However, the pub they had been booked into had served up one of the best meals Norman could ever recall eating, and this had done a lot to improve his disposition. He had even managed to convince Darling that things could only get better, although he wasn't actually convinced that was going to be the case.

After an equally satisfying breakfast, they were now on their way to speak to the police officer who had handled Jenny's case.

Detective Sergeant Steve Casey was a world-weary forty-something who had got himself into something of a rut and didn't seem to have the will to extricate himself. This particular rut involved always following the path of least resistance. It was the only way he could even begin to keep up with the workload that had slowly but surely destroyed all his enthusiasm and energy over the last few years. He no longer enjoyed his job; he endured it.

When he had first been told he had to meet with Norman to

discuss the Jane Doe case, he had been less than pleased. Up until now,
he had been the only one who knew exactly how many corners he had
cut and how many unanswered questions he had ignored. But he knew
only too well that if Norman had anything about him, he would see all
those things.

Casey should have been worried about this, but, to his great
surprise, he found he didn't seem to care. Or maybe it wasn't that he
didn't care, but that he just didn't have any energy left with which to
care. He was perhaps even slightly relieved that someone might actually see how the only way he could meet the demands placed upon him
was to cut corners and cheat the system.

He was due to meet Norman in less than five minutes, and he had
no idea what he was going to tell him. He wondered how it had all
come to this. He had been a good copper once, hoping to make a
difference, but now the only way he could keep up with the pace and
appear to be doing his job was by not doing it. How could that be
right? When had policing become a numbers game? And who was
being served by such a system? Certainly not the victims of crime.

'Well, Steve, we haven't seen the case notes,' said Norman after
they'd made the introductions. 'Can you talk us through it? Then if
we've got any questions, we can get them out of the way right now. Is it
okay if Naomi takes notes?'

'Yeah, okay,' said Casey, still undecided how he should play this
situation. He opened the file and stared at the notes. 'Right, so, the
Jane Doe--'

'We told you her name was Jenny Radstock,' Darling interrupted.

Casey glared at her. 'Right, whatever. Her body was initially found
by two police community support officers. Someone had dialled 999
and reported a body in one of the squats, and the PCSOs were sent to
check it out. Luckily it was a fresh one, or the smell would probably
have made one of them puke all over the scene.'

He looked up with a sly smile on his face, but Norman had obviously chosen not to see the funny side, and Darling simply scowled
back at him.

'Can I just remind you she was friend of ours?' said Norman
quietly.

'Right, sorry.' Casey looked back down at his notes. 'Anyway, the PCSOs called it in, and I got lumbered with going to assess the scene. When I arrived, the doctor was there, and he suggested it was a case of suicide by accidental overdose. I couldn't see any reason to question his conclusion, and my report says as much. That's about it, really.'

He sat back with a smile of relief.

'I assume you took photos of the scene?' asked Norman.

'Yeah, of course I did.' He shuffled a handful of photos from the file and slid them across the table.

Norman carefully laid them out on the table in front of them, Darling studying them alongside. 'Did you think she was a habitual junkie?' Norman asked.

'Why not?'

'Well, I'm no expert, but she looks rather well fed and dressed for a junkie, don't you think?'

Casey looked at the upside-down photos. 'I can't say I gave it much thought. When someone's got a syringe sticking out of their arm and they've injected enough heroin to put an elephant in a trance, I don't need to check the labels on their clothing to know what I'm dealing with.'

'And you're sure you were dealing with a suicide?'

'Look, mate, this is a busy patch of turf. We don't have time to fart around.'

'Fart around?' Darling echoed. 'Is that what you call it when you're investigating a death?'

Casey looked at Darling. 'I don't know what rank you were,' he said, testily, 'but you're not a copper now. Even when you were, I doubt you're old enough to have got higher than constable, so a little respect wouldn't go amiss.'

'Easy now, Steve,' said Norman. 'We're not here to judge. We just want to know the facts, that's all. Naomi's just a little touchy about drugs.'

Casey glowered at Darling, but he said nothing more.

'And Naomi also knows something that you don't know about Jenny,' added Norman.

'Oh, yeah? And what might that be?'

'She was left-handed.'

Casey shrugged. 'Yes, and?'

'And if you were left-handed, which arm would you inject into?' Norman asked.

Casey looked confused for a moment, then it dawned on him. 'Oh. Well, yeah, but I didn't know that, did I? I just assumed.'

'And we all know what happens when we assume, don't we?'

Casey now looked distinctly uncomfortable. 'But I didn't know, did I? Anyway, it's not impossible. Maybe she was ambidextrous.'

'She wasn't,' said Norman.

'The pathologist never said anything about that,' Casey snapped.

'Well, he already knows what we think of him,' said Norman.

Something had caught Darling's attention, and she pointed to one of the photographs. 'What about this pizza on the table?'

'So? It's a pizza,' said Casey.

'But five slices have been eaten.'

'And your point is?'

'My point is obvious – there was no pizza in Jenny's stomach, so who ate it?'

Casey's mouth flapped open.

'Don't you think that suggests someone could have been in that room with her?' asked Darling.

'Not necessarily,' said Casey. 'That pizza could have been there for days. Maybe she had it the night before and didn't finish it.'

'But you checked, right?' Norman asked.

'Eh?'

'You got the lab to check how fresh it was, and you checked with the pizza place to see when they delivered a pizza to that house. It would tell you how long it had been there. It's not rocket science.'

'I can't imagine anyone would deliver pizzas in that area,' said Casey. 'They probably wouldn't get paid!'

Norman looked intently at Casey. 'When you say you "can't imagine", are you saying you didn't actually check?'

'There was no point—'

'Yeah, I think I'm getting the idea.' Norman shook his head. 'What about the injuries to her leg? The pathologist suggested she had probably been hit by a car. We know she didn't go to the hospital, but did anyone report such an accident?'

Casey's mouth was working, but he seemed to have lost the power of speech.

Norman heaved a heavy sigh. 'Let's cut to the chase, shall we? Am I right in thinking you didn't make any effort to investigate anything to do with this case?'

Casey looked at the floor but said nothing.

'Let me guess – accepting it was a suicide was the easiest thing to do, right?'

Casey glared at Norman and then banged his fist on the table. 'Have you any bloody idea how much time it would take me to investigate every incident that lands on my desk?' he roared. 'Well? Have you?'

Norman stared impassively back at Casey. It was Darling who spoke. 'Actually, yes, I have. That was one of the reasons I quit.'

Casey looked surprised. 'Oh. So you understand why I took the easy way out. It's the only way I can keep on top of everything.'

'Sorry,' said Darling. 'If you're looking for sympathy you've come to the wrong girl. If you can't cope, you should ask for help or get out altogether.'

'Doing it your way just proves you're not keeping on top of everything, doesn't it?' asked Norman.

Casey's face told Norman he had obviously never thought of it like that. 'No one is given the time to worry about that, mate. It's policing by numbers. All they worry about here are crime figures and targets.'

'How do you sleep at night?' Darling asked.

'It's easy,' Casey said. 'I'm so bloody exhausted, I can hardly stay awake long enough to eat my dinner!'

Norman stared at Casey and slowly shook his head. 'I can't recall the exact wording of the oath you swore when you joined,' he said, 'but I know the words "fairness, integrity, diligence, and impartiality" are included. Now, tell me how you've applied any one of those words to this case.'

Norman gave Casey a full minute, but he didn't speak. 'Your silence sums it up pretty accurately. There's also a bit in the oath about "discharging your duties to the best of your skill and knowledge". Obviously you ignore that bit too.'

Casey was staring at the floor again and Norman sighed. 'I'm sorry,' he said. 'We really didn't come here for this. We just wanted to know what happened to Jenny, but the fact is, you can't actually tell us because you've ignored your responsibilities, right? Is the crime scene still intact?'

'Some vandals set fire to it about a week ago,' said Casey miserably.

'And even that didn't make you stop and think?' asked Darling.

'Don't you dare judge me. You have no idea--'

'Of course we have an idea. We're both police officers who recently left the service,' hissed Norman, leaning forward in his chair, his face a mask of fury. 'That means we're also in a position to judge, whether you like it or not. Naomi's right – you should have told your boss a long time ago if you can't cope.'

There was an awkward silence in the room until Darling spoke again. 'Okay,' she said, turning a page in her notebook and readying her pen. 'So how about we see what possibilities we can draw from what we do know. What do you think?'

She looked from Casey to Norman, but it was clear neither was going to offer much input at this stage. 'I'll start then, shall I?' She put pen to paper and began writing. 'Fact one: we know she was probably hit by a car a day or two before she died.

"Fact two: according to our knowledge, Jenny was not a heroin user, and the pathologist backs this up with his findings. Fact three: fact two makes it unlikely she would have injected herself with heroin. The fact she was left-handed and the syringe was found in her left arm tends to support this theory.

"Fact four: there was a half-eaten pizza in the room. It could have been there from the day before, but it could also indicate someone else was in the room before she died, or even that someone else was in the room when she died.'

She looked from Norman to Casey and back. 'Feel free to join in, won't you?'

'One conclusion,' said Norman, who had now calmed down, 'is that someone forcibly injected her with heroin and then sat eating pizza as he watched her die.'

'Jesus, do you think so?' Darling asked.

Norman pulled a face. 'We're a long way from proving it's not just pure fantasy, but it's a theory that could fit with what we know.'

Casey looked guiltily at Norman. 'It did occur to me that she might have been dealing and stepped on someone's toes.'

Darling pointed to the file on the table. 'I suppose there's nothing about that in there.'

Casey squirmed uncomfortably.

'But then I suppose including that might have involved you doing some real police work,' Darling finished.

'Did you seriously think she was dealing?' Norman asked Casey. 'Do you have any proof? I've known her a long time, and I never saw anything to suggest that. She shared a house with another police officer for a while, and he never suspected her of anything dodgy either.'

'It was just a possibility,' said Casey. 'Administer a quick overdose and Bob's your uncle. It's a popular way of dealers eliminating the competition around here.'

Norman glowered at Casey. 'But not that popular you thought you should mention it in your report.'

'Did she have any personal possessions?' asked Darling quickly. 'Mobile phone, credit cards, purse?'

'No, there was nothing like that,' said Casey.

Norman swore angrily. 'Surely that one fact, on its own, would have been enough for you to question the suicide idea! Who hides all that stuff before they take their own life? At the very least, you should have been thinking robbery.'

He glared at Casey once more for luck then stood up. 'C'mon, Naomi. Get your notes, grab that file, and let's get out of here. We can't afford to waste any more time.'

'What about me?' asked Casey miserably.

'Frankly, I couldn't give a toss about you,' said Norman. 'But maybe you should consider writing a letter to your boss.'

———

'I don't think there's much hope for law and order in Redville if Steve Casey's anything to go by,' said Darling as she started her car. 'D'you think they're all like that in there?'

'I sure hope not,' said Norman. 'In fact, I'd bet he's the only one with an attitude that bad. But it only takes one bad apple, you know?'

'Don't get me wrong,' said Darling. 'I don't feel sorry for the guy, but he does have a point about it being a numbers game.'

Norman sighed. 'Yeah, but if he's struggling to cope, he should be honest enough to say so. Faking it doesn't help anyone, does it?'

'Are you going to report him?'

'I'm not in a position to do that, but I'll let Bradshaw know. If I know him, he'll kick up a stink, but let's hope he can wait for a while.'

'Why's that? Do you want to get out of the way before the shit hits the fan?'

'Oh, I don't have a problem with alienating the locals,' said Norman, 'but if we need help at some stage, we're more likely to get it if we haven't pissed everyone off.'

'Now that's a good point,' Darling said. 'Okay, so where to?'

'Let's go back to the pub,' he said. 'I need to speak to Bradshaw, then we can have something to eat while we work out what we know and where we go next.'

CHAPTER EIGHT

Derelict was the first word that came to Norman's mind when they turned into Claremont Road. 'Are you sure this is it?' he asked.

'It's not great, is it?' said Darling. 'A little TLC certainly wouldn't hurt this place.'

'I think it's too late for TLC. I think demolition is the only solution for a place like this.'

As he spoke, a rat the size of a Jack Russell terrier ran across the road ahead of them. Norman whistled in surprise. From the corner of his eye, he saw Darling shudder, and her fingers whitened on the steering wheel.

'Oh my God,' she said. 'Was that rat?'

'Did you see the size of it?' he said gleefully. 'I swear I've seen dogs smaller than that.'

'If there are rats here, I'm not getting out,' said Darling adamantly. 'I hate rats.'

'There are rats everywhere,' said Norman. 'I read somewhere that in London, you're never more than a few feet from a rat.'

'That's as maybe,' said Darling, 'but this isn't London, and that was no ordinary rat.'

Norman grinned at her discomfort. 'Ha! I never knew you would be scared by a little rodent.'

'That was not a "little rodent". That thing was bloody humongous!'

'The rats will be more scared of you than you are of them,' Norman said sagely.

'Trust me, they couldn't possibly be,' she said. 'And I would appreciate it if you'd stop enjoying this quite so much.'

'It's just that I've never seen you scared of anything before,' he said with a wry smile.

'So now you know I'm human. Can we just get this over with?'

'Hey, you're the one who stopped the car, not me. Anyhow, we've come in from the wrong end.' He pointed to the shabby house opposite. 'This is number 93, we want 17. It'll be down the other end.'

Darling sped down to the other end of the road, coming to a stop outside number 17.

'Come on,' Norman said, opening his door.

'Not with a rat that big hanging around.'

'The rat was down the other end of the street. What do you think it's going to do, sprint down here just to scare you? Anyway, they don't "hang around" waiting for people to frighten.'

'Since when did you become the expert on rat behaviour?'

'Come on, Naomi. If this place is burnt-out like Casey said, we're only gonna be here two minutes. The sooner you quit griping and get out of the car, the sooner it'll be over with.'

'Alright,' she snapped. 'If you insist, I'll come with you, but just you remember this wasn't my idea.'

She switched the engine off, climbed from the car, and stomped round to follow him to the front door of the house.

'I think if I was a rat I'd have more sense than to get in your way,' said Norman over his shoulder. 'I've seen what you can do to a grown man.'

'That's different,' Darling said. 'I'm not scared of grown men.'

Norman stopped at the front door, raised his hand to knock on it, and then hesitated.

'What?' she asked from behind him.

'This door looks so rotten it's falling apart.'

She leaned around him for a closer look. 'I can't believe anyone actually lives inside there, can you?'

'Let's find out.'

As he knocked on the door, it swung slowly open, catching on the floor when it was about half open. A damp, musty smell seeped into their nostrils. Norman took a step back and looked up and down the road. 'Have you noticed how quiet it is along this street?'

'Yeah, it's kind of eerie,' Darling agreed.

He pushed the door open and took a step inside. 'Yo!' he called out. 'Is there anyone here?'

His voice echoed back. There was a light switch just inside the door. He didn't think for one minute that it would work, but he flicked it anyway. Nothing happened. 'This house is totally derelict,' he said.

'Even squatters would want somewhere better than this,' agreed Darling.

Norman slowly led them along the gloomy, narrow hallway of the house, the light from the open doorway just about enough to let them to see where they were going. Years of dust and grime quickly proved that Norman's assessment of the building was correct. There was a door to either side of the hallway, and a tumbledown staircase on the right.

'I'm not going up there,' said Darling.

'There's no need. It's supposed to be a downstairs room at the back,' said Norman. 'It must be that one.'

He pointed to a door a little further down on the right.

'I thought Casey said there had been a fire,' said Darling. 'Surely it would have burnt the whole house down in minutes.'

Norman reached for the door handle and put his shoulder to the door as it turned. It creaked open to reveal a charred interior, the ceiling blackened with soot. The room was open to the elements, courtesy of a smashed window at the far side of the room, the remaining shards of glass blackened with a sooty layer.

'Crap. There's nothing left to see in here,' said Norman.

'This was no accident, was it?' said Darling. 'I can't believe the whole house didn't go up.'

'Someone knew what they were doing,' said Norman. 'My guess is this fire was only supposed to destroy any evidence that might have been left in this room.'

'Can we get out of here?'

'There's nothing to stay for, is there?'

Darling scuttled back through the house and out into the fresh air, Norman following close behind.

'God, what a stink in there,' she said.

'Yeah, damp, rot, and charred fire remains. It's not exactly your regular air freshener, is it?' Norman looked up and down the street. 'This whole street's derelict, isn't it?'

'It looks like it's been like this for years,' Darling said.

'So why did Casey and the pathologist describe it as an area where users live?'

'Jenny couldn't have been living here,' said Darling. 'You've only got to look at the clothes she was wearing. There's no way she could have kept herself that smart if she was dossing here. Should we go back to Casey?'

'We'll keep that as an option,' said Norman, 'but as he's likely to give us nothing but more bullshit, I think we should first see how far we can get on our own.'

'So where do you want to start?'

'I'd like to know for sure if there was someone else in this dump on the day she died. I wanna know who it was and what they were doing there.'

'Yeah, finding whoever that is could blow the whole thing wide open,' said Darling, 'but where do we start?'

'We could try that pizza place,' Norman suggested.

'Didn't Casey say they wouldn't deliver out here?'

'Yes he did, but there's a good chance that was bull as well. It won't hurt to check for ourselves, will it?'

CHAPTER NINE

P atty's Pizza restaurant was strategically situated in a small square not far from the town centre. Patty herself was a forty-year-old bleached blonde with a sound business brain and a no-nonsense attitude.

'You buy a pizza and I'll give you five minutes of my time,' she said when they approached her. 'I think that's fair, don't you?'

Norman smiled appreciatively. He liked people who let him know where they stood right from the start. 'Yeah, that sounds totally fair.'

'We're not too busy, so I'll bring it over when it's ready.'

Norman and Darling made their way to a corner table and sat down. Norman looked around the room thoughtfully.

'What's on your mind?' asked Darling.

'I just can't see her suddenly getting into heroin, can you?'

'The pain relief idea doesn't grab you, then?'

'Does it grab you?' he asked.

'No way. If she got hit by a car, how come she didn't end up in hospital? That foot was pretty badly battered, and her leg was broken. She wasn't stupid. She would have known she needed hospital treatment.'

'Maybe we're barking up the wrong tree thinking it was a car that hit her,' said Norman. 'What was she doing in a place like that? If she was living there, why was none of her stuff there? It makes more sense to think someone had taken her there. What if you were right and those wounds were the result of a blunt instrument?'

'You think someone might have broken her leg on purpose? But why?'

'Jenny had got herself into some serious trouble. That's how she came to be living rough. We knew that much right from the start, but she never told Dave what exactly that trouble was. Suppose she knew something, and someone wanted to know what it was?'

'Or maybe she knows where something is,' said Darling. 'Perhaps she's got some incriminating evidence hidden away somewhere.'

'I think she was living somewhere in this town,' Norman said.

'Good luck finding that without anything to go on.'

'Maybe we have got something to go on. When we found her on the street, she had dyed her hair black, and she's done it again now.'

Darling shrugged. 'I don't see how that's going to help.'

'It's just a hunch, but what if she was here before and she knows people here?' Norman said. 'Maybe she was living on the street here before she came to Tinton. She might just have dyed her hair black because that's how people here would remember her.'

'I still don't see how that helps.'

'I could be completely wrong, but if she had been in touch with some of the homeless people around here, maybe they know where she's been living.'

'It sounds like a long shot,' said Darling slowly, 'but I suppose we've to nothing to lose by asking around.'

'So you'll do it then?' asked Norman.

She stared at him. 'Me? Why me?'

'Because you're young, female, good-looking, and you don't look like a cop. They'll see me as a cop, which makes me a threat, whereas there's no reason they should see you as a threat. Flash a photo of Jenny and ask around. Tell them you're her cousin and you're looking for her.'

'But you saw the clothes she was wearing,' Darling pointed out. 'She wasn't living on the street.'

'Yeah,' Norman said, 'but that doesn't mean she wasn't talking to them. Maybe she was helping them out with money or something. I'll be nearby keeping an eye on you. If there's any trouble, I'll be there.'

Darling looked doubtful, but they had nothing else to go on. 'I don't need protection,' she told him. 'I can look after myself.'

'Yes, I know, but I'll feel better if I know you're okay.'

'Can I eat my pizza first?'

Norman could see Patty approaching with their pizzas. 'Sure. Here they come now.'

'So what's this all about?' asked Patty once she had delivered their pizzas and settled alongside Darling.

Norman placed a photo of Jenny on the table. 'This woman was found dead in Claremont Road a couple of weeks ago. We're trying to find out what happened to her.'

'Was she the suicide?'

'You know about it?'

'Only what I read in the local newspaper. Didn't she overdose on heroin or something like that?'

'That's a possibility,' said Norman, 'but it's also possible that's not what really happened.'

'Are you the police?' asked Patty. 'Only I don't recall seeing your ID.'

'No, we're not police, and you don't have to talk to us if you don't want to. We're here on behalf of Jenny's parents. The police say she was a heroin user who overdosed. Her parents don't believe she was a heroin user, and nor do we. We're just trying to find the truth about what happened to her.'

Patty studied Norman's face for a few seconds. 'I've got a daughter of my own,' she said. 'She's only a teenager now, but if anything happened to her, I'd want to know as much as I could. How can I help you?'

'When she was found, there was one of your pizza boxes nearby with a half-eaten pizza. If we can find out when that pizza was delivered, it might help us pin down a more accurate time of death.'

'Did you say she was found in Claremont Road?'

'That's right.'

'Then it wouldn't have been delivered by us. We haven't delivered down there for months, not since all the slums were emptied and the squatters moved in. They don't pay, you see.'

'They can't help being homeless,' said Darling.

'I've got nothing against them being homeless, love,' said Patty. 'As a matter of fact, I supply the local homeless shelter with fresh pizzas every Tuesday night. If anyone homeless wants a free one, they can go there, but I'm not prepared to give them away any other time. I'm trying to survive as well, you know.'

'I'm sorry,' Darling said. 'I didn't mean to offend you. It's just a bit frustrating when no one seems to want to help us.'

'No offence taken,' said Patty. 'Anyway, I didn't say I wouldn't help, I just said we don't deliver out there.'

She had Norman's attention now. 'Yes, but?' he said encouragingly.

'But I did have a bit of a bust-up with some bloke who came in here demanding we deliver a pizza to Claremont Road.'

'When was this?'

'A couple of weeks ago, maybe a bit more. It was a Friday, I remember that because it was lunchtime and we're always busy Friday lunchtime. He got quite abusive about it until I threatened to call the police. That shut him up, I can tell you.'

'What happened then?'

'He calmed down, paid for his pizza, waited while we cooked it, and then took it with him.'

Norman leaned forward. 'Can you remember what sort of pizza it was?'

'I think it was just cheese, nothing exotic.'

'And it was in one of your boxes, right?'

'Oh yes,' she assured him. 'It gets our name around.'

Norman looked at Darling. He could see she was as excited as he was. 'Can you recall what this guy looked like?' he asked.

'I'm not sure I can remember exactly what he looked like,' she said, 'but I remember he was fortyish, and he was tall, well over six feet. He seemed to be head and shoulders above me. I think he was hoping he could intimidate me because he was so tall, but he got that wrong.'

'He sounds like a pretty big guy,' said Norman.

'Not that big,' said Patty. 'Oh, he was tall enough, but there was nothing of him. He was really skinny, like a beanpole.'

'Have you ever seen him before?' asked Darling.

'I don't think so.'

'Have you seen him since?'

'No, I'm sorry.'

'Don't apologise,' said Norman. 'You've been very helpful.'

'Have I? Oh, good, that's nice to know.' She looked around the restaurant, which was beginning to fill with customers seeking something to take home after work. 'I'm sorry, but I'm going to have to go.'

'Sure,' said Norman. 'Thanks again, you've been great. This pizza's really something too!'

She gave him a big smile. 'Why, thank you.' She rose from the table and began to walk away, then turned and came back. 'One more thing,' she said. 'He had a tattoo on his forearm. Some sort of dagger, I think it was.'

'Right or left arm?' asked Norman.

She thought for a moment. 'I'd say right, but I couldn't swear to it.'

'That's great, Patty,' said Norman. 'You're a star.'

CHAPTER TEN

There was a group of about ten men of varying ages sitting around a small bonfire. There were at least three who Darling thought were probably not even eighteen, and one or two around twenty. Living rough tended to age people prematurely, so after the obviously young ones, it was difficult to work out how old anyone else really was.

One of the youngsters spotted her first. She couldn't make out what he said, but soon all eyes were turned her way as she approached. It said a lot for Darling's confidence in her ability to defend herself that she didn't for one moment consider she might have been at risk.

A surly-looking man seemed to be their leader, and now he stepped forward to intercept her.

'Hi,' she said, loud enough for them all to hear. 'I'm sorry to disturb you guys. I'm looking for someone, and I was hoping one of you might be able to help me.'

'Which one of us?' asked Surly Man.

She was momentarily thrown by his question, but quickly recovered. 'I don't mean any particular one of you, just anyone who might recognise a face in a photo.'

'Are you the law?' asked Surly Man. 'Cos if you are, you can piss off. We ain't done nothing wrong.'

'No,' said Darling indignantly, 'I am not "the law", as you put it.'

'Why should we help you then?'

'Would you help me if I was "the law"?'

'Course not. Why would we? What do they do for us? Nothing, except give us grief. They say we're makin' the place look untidy, like we're litter. They seem to forget we're human beings, so sod 'em, that's what I say.'

'So it wouldn't make any difference if I was "the law", or not,' said Darling. 'You wouldn't help anyway.'

'Why should we?'

'How about because I'm here looking for my cousin? I was told she was here in town somewhere, but I haven't been able to find her, and I'm worried about her. I was hoping one of you might have seen her.'

'What's in it for us?' Surly Man asked.

'Apart from the satisfaction of doing someone a good deed? Well, I would imagine you could all do with a good, hot meal.'

A sneaky smile creased the man's face. 'Well, if you're paying for information I can probably help you.'

Darling smiled back at him. 'I wasn't born yesterday, you know, so don't think you're going to give me any old crap. I'll pay, but only if the information is good.'

Surly Man stepped forward and glowered at her. 'I don't think you're in a position to be makin' threats, little girl.'

He reached for her arm, but she was much too quick for him, and before he knew it he was on his backside, looking rather stupid. 'Why, you little bitch,' he hissed. 'I'll get you for this.'

'I don't think so,' said a voice behind him.

'Who the f-- Ah! Jesus! You're standing on my bloody hand.'

'Am I?' asked Norman innocently. He looked down at his foot. 'Oh yeah, you're right, I am. Sorry about that. I didn't see it in the dark. Good job I lost some weight or that coulda really hurt.'

Just to emphasise the point, he put little more weight on the hand before he moved his foot, then he grabbed Surly Man by the scruff of the neck and hauled him to his feet.

'You probably think you're pretty hard, but you should think your-self lucky,' Norman hissed in his ear. 'If I hadn't come along, she probably woulda beat the crap out of you, and that would make you look even more stupid in front of your crew here, wouldn't it?'

'Oh, I get it,' said the man. 'You've just come here for some sport, have you? Pick on the down-and-outs?'

'No, it isn't,' snapped Darling. 'I told you, all I want to do is show you a photo of my friend and ask if anyone has seen her. You're the one who wanted to make it into something else.'

'Well, tell your gorilla to take his hands off me and maybe I'll help you. It'll cost you, mind.'

'How much?'

'A ton!'

Norman guffawed. 'Come on, let's get out of here. This guy's having a laugh.'

'It's a fair price!' argued Surly Man.

'And I suppose you want all the money?'

'Well, yeah, of course I do. I'll share it out.'

'What you mean,' Darling said, 'is you'll stuff it into your pocket, and the other guys'll get nothing.'

He glared at her but said nothing.

'I'll tell you how this is going to work. I'll show you all a photograph. Everyone who looks at it will get a tenner. Anyone who has information will get more. Okay?'

'I decide what happens here,' snapped Surly.

Norman yawned. 'Look, pal, that's our final offer. You can take it or leave it.'

He scowled at Norman. 'I ought to kick your head in,' he muttered.

'Yeah, but you already tried that, and ended up on your arse,' said Norman, 'so it's probably not a good idea. We already told you we didn't come here looking for a fight, so why don't you calm down and accept our offer? Ten quid each has to be better than nothing, right?'

'Piss off,' said Surly, and stormed off into the darkness.

Norman turned to the other guys, who were watching, open-mouthed. 'Anyone else want to walk away? No? Okay, come take look at the photo and see if you can help us.'

Darling produced a torch and shone it on the photograph so each of them could see it properly. Each one took their ten-pound note, but no one admitted they knew who the girl in the photo was. No one would own up to knowing a tall, skinny man with a dagger tattoo either.

One young lad called Spiderhair, who had wild, curly hair that was being kept under control by a large woolly hat, seemed to be on the verge of admitting he knew her, but then seemed to change his mind.

'That kid with the crazy hair knows something,' said Darling as they walked away.

'Yeah, I thought so too,' said Norman. 'I wonder why he wouldn't say anything.'

'He's the smallest. Perhaps he's frightened the others will steal any extra money we might give him.'

'You could be right. Maybe we'll try finding him tomorrow and ask him again.'

They were almost back into the centre of town when a shadowy figure stepped out in front of them. Darling was so startled she almost launched herself at him, but Norman put a hand out to stop her.

'Wait,' he said. 'It's okay. It's Spiderman.'

'You want to be careful,' said Darling to the boy in front of her. 'You jump out in front of people like that and sooner or later someone is going to give you a good hiding.'

Spiderhair looked sheepish. 'Sorry,' he said. 'It's that girl in the photo. I know her.'

'I thought you did,' said Norman. 'Why didn't you say back there?'

'If Jasper knows I've got money, he'll kick the crap out of me until he gets it.'

'I take it Jasper's the mouthy guy we humiliated back there.'

'Yeah, that's right.'

'Is he the leader of your little gang?'

'Only because he's got control of the fire. There aren't many places round here you can get warm at night, and he knows it.'

'Sounds like a nice guy.'

'He's not all bad. He can be alright sometimes.'

'Aren't you worried he's gonna figure out you're talking to us and getting the money?' Norman asked.

'He'll guess I've come after you, but he won't know where I am. If I can keep out of his way tonight, I can stash the money in my savings account in the morning.'

'You have a savings account?' asked Norman in surprise.

'I'm saving up to get out of here,' said the boy. 'I don't wanna spend the rest of my life like this. If I can save enough, I can pay to go back to college.'

'Wow! That's a pretty cool sort of ambition to have,' said Norman. 'I hope it works out for you.'

'Have you eaten lately?' Darling asked.

'Living like this, you have to eat when you get the chance.'

'Think you can manage fish and chips?' asked Norman.

'Cor, yeah, please.'

'What's your real name? We can't keep calling you Spiderhair.'

'Neil. It's a bit dull, isn't it? Spiderhair's a lot more fun.'

'Hey, I'm a dull Norman. I think Neil is just fine.'

'Well, I'm stuck with it, whether I like it or not.'

'Why do they call you Spiderhair?' asked Darling.

'Tada!' he said, as he whipped his woolly hat off. His hair seemed to spring out in all directions, like coiled springs just released. 'Someone used to tell me it looked like spiders' legs gone wild.'

Norman grinned his appreciation. His own hair had a similar tendency if he didn't keep it cut short. 'Right,' he said. 'I kinda see what they mean.'

'That's why I wear the hat.'

'I can definitely see the need,' said Darling.

————

'Yeah, I know her,' said Spiderhair, looking at the photo again. They were sitting on a bench under a street light, a short distance from the chip shop. He stuffed a handful of chips into his mouth and chewed hungrily.

'How come you know her?' asked Darling.

'I met her months ago,' he said. 'She called herself Ginger.'

Norman knew Jenny had used that name when she was living rough. 'That's right, she did. How did you meet?'

'She was living on the street when I arrived here. Nice she was, although she never took no shit from anyone. She looked out for me, a bit like a big sister. She's the one who christened me Spiderhair. Then one day she disappeared, just like that. Never told anyone she was going. I was bit pissed off, I can tell you.'

'Did she leave you in some sort of trouble?'

'Nah, it wasn't that. I just sort of got used to her being there, you know? I think I fancied her a bit as well, not that I had any sort of chance, but a kid can dream, right?' He looked shyly at Norman, who smiled back at him.

'We've all had dreams like that,' said Norman. 'And it would be a pretty dull life without dreams, that's for sure.'

'Do you know why she turned up here again?' asked Darling.

'Now, you've got me there,' Spiderhair said. 'She was like a different person, all cleaned up, wearing nice clothes. Even her hair was its natural colour when I first saw her, you know? Coming back here made no sense to me. When I finally get away from here, I shan't be thinking about coming back, not in a million years.'

'So you were surprised to see her?'

'Shocked, more like. She said she'd come back to see me. She had money too. She gave me nearly two hundred quid to put into my savings account.'

'That was good of her,' said Darling.

'Yeah. She said it was to make up for leaving me in the shit, like. I said she didn't need to do it, but she insisted. That was the last time I saw her, actually.'

He had finished his fish and chips and was now slurping his way through a huge coffee.

'How long ago was that?' asked Norman.

'I haven't seen her for about three weeks now.'

'And you have no idea where she went?'

'Nah, not a clue. It's the same as last time. She just disappeared again.'

'Do you know where she was staying when she was here?' asked Norman.

'Nah, she never said.'

'What about a name? Maybe she was staying with a friend or something?'

'She did mention a couple of names once, but she liked a joke, you know? I think she was probably taking the piss.'

'Why's that?' asked Darling.

Spiderhair laughed. 'How many Ben and Jerrys do you know?'

'You mean like the ice cream guys?'

'Yeah, exactly,' he said. 'It's not likely, is it?'

'She didn't mention a street or anything that might give us clue?'

'Just Ben and Jerry. I got a feeling it might even have been something from her past. Can I ask a question?'

'Sure,' said Norman.

'You know Ginger, don't you?'

'Yeah,' Norman admitted. 'But I knew her as Jenny. She stayed with a friend of mine for a while.'

'Oh, right. Well, if you find her, can you tell her hello from Spiderhair?'

Norman looked at Darling. He was wondering if they should tell him the truth about Jenny. 'Yeah, sure,' he said, after a moment's hesitation. 'If we find her we'll do that.'

'One more thing,' said Darling. 'I know we already asked, but did you ever see her with a tall, skinny guy with a dagger tattooed on his arm.'

'No, sorry. I can't ever recall seeing her with a bloke like that.'

'Okay, Neil, well thanks for your help,' said Norman. He counted out five twenty-pound notes and handed them to the boy. 'This is our contribution to your college fund. Make sure you keep saving.'

'Oh, wow, how cool is that?' said Spiderhair, stuffing the money into his coat pocket. 'Well, thanks for the food, and for the cash. You know where to find me if you need me, right?'

He gave them a jaunty wave of his right hand, then stuffed both hands deep into the pockets of his coat and walked off into the night.

'You could have told him,' said Darling as they watched him cross the street and then disappear around a corner.

'I know. I was in two minds,' said Norman. 'But he lives on the street. I can't believe he doesn't already know someone was found dead.'

'Maybe he hasn't joined the dots yet, or if he's nursing some sort of fantasy about her, perhaps he just doesn't want to believe it was her.'

'It could be that,' said Norman, 'or it could be he's just finding out what we know so he can report back to someone else.'

'D'you think so?'

'Actually, I hope I'm wrong and he's genuine, and I also hope he saves enough money to get himself out of here. But the cynic in me is telling me he could be playing us so he has information to sell on to someone else.'

'Since when did you become Mr Negative?' Darling asked.

'I'm not,' said Norman, 'but I am Mr Realist, and I know living on the street often distorts a person's moral compass. It's a survival thing, I guess.'

CHAPTER ELEVEN

'Well, whaddyaknow?' said Norman as he joined Darling for breakfast next morning. 'I've just been speaking to Bradshaw. We finally got some luck going our way.'

'Does he know our mysterious stranger with the tattoo?'

'No, he has no ideas on that score, but he tells me Jenny's mobile phone has been switched on.'

Darling stopped with her fork halfway to her mouth. 'Wow! Did they get a trace on it?'

'Yeah, it's in town here. He's sending me a map.'

'Does he have any idea who's using it?'

'Wouldn't that be something? Sadly, it was only switched on for a minute or so, and we're lucky to have what we have. They know it's the right handset by its ID number, but it's got an unused pay-as-you-go SIM card loaded so that's no help to anyone. Luckily, they were looking for the actual handset and not her number or they might have missed it altogether.'

'Doesn't it make you wonder why now?' asked Darling. 'It's been weeks since she last used it, and she's been dead for over two weeks.'

'We always assumed she hadn't used it because she thought there might be a watch on it,' said Norman. 'I even thought she might have dumped it somewhere.'

'Perhaps she did and someone found it. But if it's whoever murdered her, and he was after information, why wait until now?'

'Maybe she hid it, and they've just found it,' Norman mused. 'Or maybe someone stole it when she died and decided to wait until the heat had died down.'

'But why change the SIM card?' Darling asked. 'If they wanted contact details, that's probably where they were stored!'

Norman shrugged and they were silent for a moment. 'We can sit here and speculate until the cows come home,' he said finally, 'but the only way we're going to find out for sure is to go and find whoever has it and ask some questions.'

'You know, you're right, Norm. Now I understand why you think you're the boss around here,' Darling said, laughing.

'Let's just hope we can find that damned phone,' he replied, 'or it won't matter who's the boss.'

———

After breakfast, using the information provided by Bradshaw, they used Norman's mobile phone to open the map. Then they drove into town, parked as close as they could to the spot, and walked the final hundred yards or so.

'It should be just around this corner,' said Norman at last.

'Damn! This can't be right,' said Darling as they turned the corner and found themselves in a narrow pedestrian alleyway just a few feet wide.

'It's a good job we didn't bring the car any further,' said Norman. 'We would have looked pretty stupid trying to turn down here!' He squinted at his map.

'I thought you were an expert with that phone,' said Darling over his shoulder. 'Isn't that what you told me?'

'And your point is?'

'The map. Try enlarging it,' she suggested.

'I knew that,' he said, embarrassed. 'I was just going to.'

'Yeah, of course you were.'

He fiddled with the phone, enlarged the map, and studied it again. 'Ah! Don't panic,' he said. 'This leads through to the shopping centre.' He pointed to the wall beside them. 'Maybe the place we want is the other side of this wall.'

Darling gave him a wry smile. 'Of course, it could be the other side of that wall.' She pointed to the opposite wall.

'Okay, smarty-pants, maybe it is,' he said with a wry smile of his own, 'but because I'm in charge, we'll try my side first.'

He led the way down the alleyway until they turned left onto the main pedestrian access to the shopping centre. 'It's gotta be down at the far end there,' he said, pointing off to his left.

They walked past shops in varying sizes, some huge, well-known names, and smaller, more local shops. As they got deeper into the centre, there were fewer and fewer customers, and the shops seemed to take on a rather tired appearance, almost as if they'd been forgotten by everyone.

'That's got to be it,' said Darling. 'There, in the corner.'

On the inside of the grubby shop window, someone had scrawled in wobbly letters the words 'Terry's mobiles, gadjits, vinyls, 'n' stuff. I buy, sell, and repair'.

'They say the art of signwriting is dying because of technology,' opined Norman, pointing at the sign. 'I suggest illiteracy might just have something to do with it too.'

'You're out of touch, Norm,' said Darling. 'That's called artistic licence.'

'Artistic licence my arse. There's nothing artistic about that!'

Laughing, Darling pushed her way into the shop, Norman trailing along behind her. As the door opened, the incessant, pounding beat of dance music almost drove them backwards.

A small boy was behind the counter, his back to them as he bent over a side table and worked a keyboard. As he worked, he danced to the music, oblivious to his new customers. Darling thought he was pretty nimble on his feet, even though his timing left a lot to be desired. Norman thought it would be good if someone took a hammer to the source of the music.

'Why does it have to be so loud?' he complained.

'I'm sorry, the music's so loud I can't hear you,' she shouted.

'Yes,' he yelled. 'That's what I was saying! Why does it have to be so loud?'

The last part of the sentence was shouted into silence as the boy, realising he had visitors, turned the music off. 'Cos it's the only way to listen to it,' he said, turning and smiling at Norman.

'I'm sorry?' said Norman.

'So, the music. It's gotta be loud enough to feel it or there's no point, see?'

'No, I don't think I do. Isn't there a point where it's so loud it damages your hearing?'

The boy reached his hands up to his ears and removed an ear plug from each ear. 'That's what these are for!'

Norman scratched his head. 'But wouldn't turning the volume down achieve the same thing without deafening everyone else?'

'So, then I wouldn't be able to feel it, would I? You gotta have it loud enough to make things shake. That's when you really feel the good vibrations, see?'

'Somehow, when the Beach Boys released "Good Vibrations" I don't think this was quite what they had in mind,' said Norman.

'So, who are these Beach Boys, then?'

Norman was beginning to wish he hadn't started this, and there was one thing that he was finding particularly irritating. 'Is every sentence you utter going to begin with "so"?' he asked, his tone becoming distinctly prickly.

'Eh?'

Darling decided it was time to intervene before Norman really got into his stride. She stepped forward and smiled at the boy. 'Ignore my old dad,' she said, turning on the charm. 'He's feeling his age today, and it's making him even more grouchy than normal.'

The boy grinned back at her. 'It's cool. I get a lot of party poopers. I can handle it. My dad's just as bad, that's why I spend most of my time here in my shop.'

Norman bristled at the suggestion he was a party pooper.

'This is your shop, is it?' asked Darling, looking around dubiously. The shelves were mostly empty, and the whole place needed a good clean and a coat of paint.

'So, I know it's not much yet. I'm still waiting for most of my stock to arrive, but it'll be really cool when I get it cleaned up and done out the way I want.'

'D'you run it all on your own?'

He smiled shyly. 'Yeah, it's just me. But even Richard Branson started small, right? And look where he is now.'

'That's your dream, is it?' asked Darling. 'You want to be the next Richard Branson.'

'No, not want to be,' said the boy. 'I'm going to be. Just watch this space and you'll see.'

'What's your name? I need to know so I can watch out for you in the future.'

'Terry Davey.'

Darling reached a hand across the counter. Davey hesitated, then reached for it. 'I'm pleased to meet you,' she said as she shook his hand. 'My name's Naomi, and this is Norm.'

Norman smiled sheepishly and nodded to Davey.

'How can I help you?' asked Davey. 'If you're looking for vinyl records, that's the one thing I have got plenty of.'

He pointed to several battered cardboard boxes which appeared to be packed with old vinyl albums. On another occasion, Norman might have been tempted to browse, but they were here for a more important reason.

'I might come back and look at those another time,' he said, 'but right now what I'm really looking for is a mobile phone.'

'Ah! So, I haven't actually got any in stock yet,' said Davey. 'The suppliers are messing me around.'

'I don't want a new one,' said Norman. 'I was rather hoping you might have a used one.'

'I'm not really open for business right now.' Davey looked puzzled. 'I'm just trying to get the place ready to go.'

'But you do deal in used phones, right?' asked Norman.

'Well, yeah, sometimes.'

'What I'm looking for is a used smartphone.'

'I can keep an eye out for one, and let you know when I've got it.'

'I'm looking for a particular one,' said Norman. 'It's silver, in a pink leather case with a daisy embroidered on the front.'

Davey's eyes narrowed, and he flicked a glance at Darling, then at the door, then back at Norman.

'You're looking nervous, Davey,' said Norman. 'Now, why is that?'

'Who, me? I'm not nervous,' he said, his eyes flicking to the door again.

'Did you steal the phone?' asked Darling.

'I-I dunno what you're talking about,' Davey stammered. 'Who are you people? I think you should leave.'

'We're not going to hurt you, if that's what you think,' said Darling soothingly.

'We just want to know where you got the phone,' added Norman. 'Did you steal it?'

'No. I didn't steal anything. I don't ever steal stuff. Why do old farts like you think anyone my age must be a criminal?'

'So you admit you have the phone,' said Norman.

'I'm not admitting anything, and you can't prove--'

'We know that phone was switched on last night,' said Darling, 'and if you know anything about mobile phones, you'll know it would have pinged the nearest masts. We've had a trace on it for weeks ever since the owner went missing. As soon as it pinged, we got a trace, and we tracked it right here, to your shop.'

Davey's eyes widened, and he turned rather pale. 'Shit!' he said, his voice almost a whisper. 'Who are you?'

'We're working with the police,' said Darling. 'The girl who owned that phone went missing a few weeks ago. Obviously if we can find the phone, it might tell us where she is, or at least give us a clue about what happened to her.'

'I didn't steal it,' Davey insisted. 'Someone brought it in yesterday. He wanted cash for it, but it had a broken screen and it looked a bit battered. I said I'd buy it, but only if he left it with me so I could see if I could fix it.'

'You buy phones off anyone who walks in?' asked Norman. 'How d'you know they're not stolen?'

'How can anyone prove it _is_ stolen? You'd be surprised how many phones get lost every day. People bring them to me, I clean them up and then sell them as second-hand goods.'

'Handling stolen goods is a criminal offence, you know,' said Norman.

'But I don't know they're stolen.'

'Oh, I think you do, and I'm pretty sure a jury would think the same.'

'A jury?' Davey stared at Norman. 'What are you saying?'

'I think what he's saying is we could report you for handling stolen mobile phones,' said Darling. 'But perhaps it doesn't have to come to that.'

'What does that mean?' asked Davey desperately.

'Look, we didn't come here to frighten you.'

'But that's exactly what you are doing!'

'Yes, I'm sorry about that.'

'Are you going to arrest me?'

'We're not here to arrest anyone,' said Darling. 'We're just trying to find that mobile phone. Do you still have it?'

'And you promise you won't arrest me?'

'Promise.'

Davey reached under the counter and produced a mobile phone, which he placed down in front of them. 'I had to take it out of the case to fix the screen. And I had to switch it on to make sure it worked.'

'And does it work?' asked Norman.

'As far as I can tell, but I only tested to make sure it booted up okay. If you traced it, that means it must be sending out a signal.'

'I just wanna look and see if there's anything that might help us find her,' said Norman.

'Trust me, there's nothing on there,' said Davey. 'I wiped everything off and reset it to the original factory settings. It's the first thing I do with every second-hand phone I get.'

'But it was only on for a minute!' Norman said. 'That wouldn't have been long enough to do a reset.'

Davey gave Norman a lopsided grin. 'There are ways of blocking that signal, you know.'

'Please tell me you're kidding.' The disappointment was clear in Norman's voice.

'No. I'm serious. It wouldn't be right to sell a phone with someone else's info on there, would it?'

'Crap! What about the SIM card? Have you still got that?'

'Sorry. I destroy them. It's because of data protection and all that stuff.'

Norman raised an eyebrow. 'Forgive me for being cynical, but I find it rather ironic that a guy who handles stolen phones would claim to be worried about data protection.'

'I'm just trying to do the right thing,' said Davey indignantly.

'You'd be doing the right thing if you stopped handling stolen phones,' Norman replied, bitterly. He turned away from Davey and walked over to the shop window where he stopped and stared miserably out at the world.

Darling looked at the phone and then at Davey. 'D'you mind if I take look?'

'Be my guest,' he said, 'but I'm telling you the truth. There's nothing on it.'

Darling turned on the phone and had a quick look through it. Davey was right; it had been reset. She handed the phone back to him. 'Okay, so there's nothing on the phone, but what about the guy who brought it in? Do you know where he found it?'

'No, he didn't say.'

'Do you know where we can find him?'

Davey shrugged. 'He's just some homeless guy. I used to have a market stall, that's where I first met him, but now I've got the shop, he comes here. He's brought me a few phones over the past few months.'

'Does he have a name?'

'Spiderman, or something like that.'

Norman swung round. 'Does he have wild frizzy hair? Wears a woolly hat to keep it under control?'

'That's him,' said Davey. 'Do you know him?'

'Oh yes, we've met. Is he coming back here to get paid?'

'Yeah, he said he'd be coming today.'

Norman glanced at his watch. 'Do you know what time?'

'He didn't say.'

'In that case, we'll just have to wait for him.'

Davey looked mildly panicked. 'Not here, you can't wait here!'

'No, we're not gonna wait here, but I'll tell you something else – if you see him before us, you're not going to tell him we've been in here asking about that phone.'

Davey licked his lips, his eyes darting to Darling, and back to Norman.

'Of course, if you want me to go and speak to the local police . . .'

'No, please, you don't want to do that!' Davey cried.

'Part of me really does want to, actually,' said Norman.

'But I'll make sure he doesn't,' Darling reassured Davey, 'as long as you don't tell Spiderhair we were here, and you stop handling stolen phones.'

'Yeah, but–'

'You seem to be quite a switched-on young guy,' said Darling, 'but you don't seem to be able to see what you're doing is wrong. You could make a go of this little business if you really want to. Why spoil it for yourself?'

Now Davey looked guilty.

'You know I'm right,' Darling said finally, then she turned to Norman and headed for the door. 'Come on, Norm, I think we're done here.'

As they walked away from Davey's shop, Norman muttered, 'I'm going to be seriously pissed off if that Spiderhair kid stole that phone. I told you I wasn't convinced about him.'

Darling patted his arm as they walked. 'Let's not jump to conclusions. He might have found the phone.'

'Yeah, right,' said Norman, 'and I bet he's "found" all the other phones he's brought this guy too.'

'I've never known you to be quite this cynical.'

'Let's just look at what we have here,' said Norman. 'A young woman in her prime dies in pretty weird circumstances, leaving a lot of unanswered questions, and no one seems to give a rat's arse about it. I think that gives me pretty good reason to be cynical.'

'It's because you knew her, isn't it?' asked Darling.

'Yeah, I guess you're right,' he admitted 'This is personal, and now I wanna know what happened more than ever.'

CHAPTER TWELVE

There were two ways to get to Davey's shop, but whichever way Spiderhair chose, he would have to go through the main square of the shopping centre. It was a huge open atrium where weary customers could sit and enjoy a cup of coffee. Norman and Darling had positioned themselves at a table where they could watch both ways. They had been there nearly two hours before Darling finally spotted him.

'Here he comes,' she said. 'Looking like he hasn't got a care in the world.'

'Has he seen us?' asked Norman, not daring to swing round and give them away.

'No. He has no idea we're here. Do you want to stop him now or wait until he comes out?'

'I'm not sure I can trust Davey to keep his mouth shut,' said Norman. 'I think it might be better to stop him before he gets there.'

Darling looked around. 'It's a bit public.'

'Yeah, I know, but he thinks you're cool, right? How about if you were to go across, bump into him, and invite him over for a coffee?'

'What do you mean "he thinks I'm cool"?'

'Yeah, I probably shoulda said he thinks you're "fit". That's what kids say these days, isn't it?'

Darling was blushing. 'He does not!'

Norman laughed. 'Sure he does. I might be getting on a bit, but I'm still a guy, and I can tell exactly what he thinks about you. It was there, all over his face, last night.'

'That's complete crap, Norm.'

'Look, we can argue about it later. If you don't get a move on, we'll miss him.'

'You're talking bollocks,' Darling said as she got to her feet and started walking.

Norman turned to watch as she headed towards Spiderhair, waving to catch his attention. He was right, of course; as soon as the boy saw her, he changed direction and headed straight for her. Like putty in her hands, he followed her over to join Norman.

'Have you got time for coffee?' Norman asked.

'Too right, man,' said Spiderhair. 'I've got as long as you want. It's not as if I have to be anywhere else, is it?'

He sat down in the chair next to Darling while Norman caught the attention of a waitress and ordered three more coffees. They spent the next five minutes on idle chat, asking Spiderhair how he passed his time, where he ate, etc., but once the boy was settled and comfortable, Norman cut to the chase.

'Someone told me some of you guys make money by stealing phones and selling them on.'

Spiderhair looked surprised. 'Not me, mate.'

'I have a friend who has a shop,' said Norman. 'He tells me you bring him mobile phones.'

'Yeah? Well, first of all he shouldn't have told you anything without asking me, and second, he shoulda told you I only bring them to him when I find them. I don't nick stuff, right?'

'Just the other day you took him a phone,' said Darling. 'It was silver, in a pink leather case with a daisy embroidered on the front.'

'That's right, but I found it! I didn't nick it.'

'Are you sure about that?' asked Norman.

'Course I'm sure. I'll show you where I found it if you don't believe me. What's so important about it, anyway?'

'Remember we were talking about Ginger last night? The phone you found is hers.'

Spiderhair's eyes widened, and he looked from Norman to Darling and back. 'You're kidding me! How weird is that? But it was broken. I had no idea whose it was. I wasn't even sure it could be fixed. Shit! If I'd known it was Ginger's, I would have kept it until I saw her again.'

Darling looked at Norman and nodded towards Spiderhair, her meaning crystal clear. 'Yeah, about that,' said Norman, carefully, 'I probably should have told you yesterday.'

'What? What should you have told me?'

'I'm sorry, but Ginger's dead.'

The boy looked stunned. Darling put a consoling hand on his arm, and for a moment it seemed Spiderhair would manage to keep the tears at bay, but then, very slowly, his face began to crumple, and a single tear eased its way down his cheek. Then, as Darling reached across and pulled him to her, the dam burst and the tears began to flow in earnest.

While Spiderhair continued to sob inconsolably, Norman wondered what to make of this situation. If there had been any doubt in his mind about how this kid had really thought about Jenny, or Ginger, as he knew her, it was now painfully obvious he was very fond of her. It was hard to believe he would have stolen her phone.

Norman sighed and looked up at the atrium roof, as though hoping to find inspiration. He wondered if maybe they had arrived on the scene just a little too late. It seemed someone had gone to great lengths to make sure there was no evidence for them to find, and he was beginning to feel as though they were up the proverbial creek without a paddle.

Or were they? If Spiderhair was telling the truth about Jenny's phone, maybe they could learn something from where he had found it.

Darling was talking quietly to the boy, who now seemed to have recovered some of his composure. 'He wants to know what happened to her,' she told Norman.

'Yeah, don't we all,' said Norman.

'Can I tell him?'

'I suppose it can't do any harm.'

Darling told the boy the official police version of events. As she spoke, Spiderhair looked more and more confused. When she had finished, he turned to Norman. 'That's not right,' he said indignantly. 'They've got that all wrong. Ginger was no junkie! She never touched drugs. She was always telling me how I should make sure I never got involved. She said there was no escape once you started.'

'That's more or less what we thought,' said Norman, wondering how much he should tell the kid.

'Is that why you were asking all those questions about where she was?'

'Can you keep this conversation to yourself?'

'You have to learn how to keep a secret the way I live,' said Spiderhair. 'You tell people too much and the next thing you know, everybody knows and they all want a piece of it.'

Norman considered for a moment and then came to a decision. 'The person we're working for doesn't believe Ginger's death was an accident, and we're trying to find out what really happened.'

'If it wasn't an accident, are you saying she was murdered?'

'That's what we're trying to figure out.'

'So who are you working for?'

'It's a long story,' said Norman.

'Are you the police?'

'Not exactly,' said Darling. 'We're detectives, but we're not part of the police.'

'Can I help?' Spiderhair asked eagerly.

'I dunno,' said Norman doubtfully. 'We don't know what we're dealing with, or who we're dealing with. We wouldn't want to put you at risk.'

'But I know my way around this town, and I notice things. I could work undercover for you.'

Norman smiled. The kid meant well, but he was way too naive. 'I'm not sure we need someone undercover, but I'll bear you in mind if we do. There is something you can do, though.'

'Yeah? What's that?'

'Can you show us where you found her phone?'
'Of course I can, if you think it'll help.'

———

'J ust there, by that lamppost,' said Spiderhair, pointing over
Darling's shoulder from the back seat of her car.

Norman looked around as Darling brought the car to a halt.
He'd been expecting to be taken to another squat like the one in which
Jenny's body had been found, but this was just a normal street in a
normal, middle-class, suburban area, nothing like he had been
expecting.

'Is this it?' he asked in surprise. 'Which house?'

'I wasn't in a house,' said Spiderhair, indignantly. 'I told you, I'm
not a thief. I found the phone just lying in the grass behind that
lamppost.'

'I didn't mean to suggest you'd broken into a house. I just kinda
thought you would have been inside a house to find the phone. Out in
the open like this, we haven't got a chance of finding any clues.'

'It was just lying there in the grass,' explained a crestfallen Spiderhair. 'I'm sorry if that's not what you want to hear, but that's what
happened.'

Darling gave Norman a disappointed look. 'We could at least get
out and have look,' she said. 'He didn't have to come out here to show
us where he found it. A little gratitude wouldn't hurt, would it?'

Norman's face reddened. 'I'm sorry, I'm not blaming anyone, it's
just that I was hoping there might have been some evidence that
might help us.'

'We're here now, so let's take look.' Darling opened her door. As
she stepped out of the car, she spoke to Spiderhair. 'Can you remember
exactly when you found it?'

'It would have been a Monday morning,' he said. 'I always come for
a walk out this way on Monday mornings.'

'Where do you walk to?' Norman asked.

'Nowhere in particular. I just walk for the sake of walking. I have to
get away from the others or they'd do my head in. It was Jasper who

suggested it. He takes himself off most days, often for the whole day. He says it's one way to stop the people around you driving you mental. So I tried it for a week, and he was right, so now I go off for a walk most mornings. Mondays, I come out this way.'

'And you found it where, exactly?' asked Darling.

'Just there, in the grass at the back of that lamppost.' He pointed to the base of the post. 'I could see the screen was busted, so I figured someone must have dropped it, but there was no one around so I picked it up and put it in my pocket.'

Norman looked along the road. About sixty yards away, a large black dog studiously sniffed the assorted canine aromas at the foot of another lamppost, his owner waiting patiently for him to complete his investigation. As Norman watched, the dog finished his inspection, cocked a leg to add a generous contribution of his own, and then man and dog ambled on towards them.

Norman turned and looked the other way. There were a few houses along here, but they were all big, expensive-looking, and detached, with tall fences and hedges to protect their privacy and stop people looking in. That also prevented people in the houses from looking out onto the road. If there had been any sort of incident out here, the chances were none of the residents would have seen a thing.

About twenty yards back from where they were, a footpath led off to the right between the houses. Norman walked back to take a look. He saw the lane went back about twenty yards and then bent to the left. He walked up to the bend and from there, he could see the lane connected with another, similar road. He walked back to join the others.

'Anything?' asked Darling.

'Nothing useful, just a footpath that connects this road with the one running parallel,' he said.

'D'you guys mind if I head off now?' asked Spiderhair. 'They do free tea and cakes at the church in town, and I said I'd meet a couple of the guys there.'

'I can drive you back,' Darling offered.

'No, that's alright. I'm still bit upset, to tell the truth. I think a walk might clear my head, you know?'

'If you're sure?'

'Thanks for the offer, but I'll be fine, honest.' He started to walk away.

'You take care, now,' called Norman. 'We'll maybe catch up with you later.'

The boy turned, nodded his head, waved his hand, and then disappeared up the alleyway. Norman turned his attention to the foot of the lamppost and the area immediately around it. 'I bet if there was any evidence anywhere around here, the local dogs would have peed all over it by now.'

'Spiderhair could have done without you giving him such a hard time,' said Darling.

Norman sighed. 'I think you kinda made that point already.'

'D'you think I'm wrong?'

'No, probably not,' he said. 'I suppose I'm just getting frustrated that we've obviously stumbled onto something much bigger than I expected, but we're getting nowhere fast.'

'Do you think Bradshaw knows about all this?'

'I'm sure he knows more than he's letting on, but I think I know him pretty well. I can't believe he'd be involved in her death or in covering it up.'

'Forgive me if I reserve judgement on that,' said Darling.

'That's fine,' said Norman. 'I told you from the start, I asked you here to be objective.'

They studied the ground around the lamppost in silence for a few seconds until a voice interrupted their thoughts. 'Are you looking for something in particular?'

They looked around together. The man and his black dog had finally reached them.

Norman smiled ruefully. 'I wish I knew,' he said.

The man looked puzzled. 'Are you the police? You're a bit late if you are. It's well over two weeks since I reported that accident.'

Norman and Darling exchanged a glance. He could see she obviously had no idea what the man was talking about either, but he had a hunch they should just play along.

'Oh, so you must be Mr, er—'

'Hancock. James Hancock.'

'That's right, Mr Hancock,' said Norman. 'Can you just run it by me again?'

'I told them at the time—'

'I understand,' said Norman patiently, 'but trust me, you might just recall something you didn't mention before. Please?'

For a moment, Norman thought Hancock was going to refuse, but then Darling bent down and started fussing the dog and, like magic, that immediately seemed to change his mood.

'I always walk my dog down to the newsagents first thing every morning, and most mornings we see this woman jogging. I think she must come out of town along Derby Road, then she comes down the connecting alleyway there, turns left, and heads back into town.'

'Can you describe her?'

'I usually just see the back of her from a distance, but I think she was about fortyish, slim, five feet four, dark hair. She always had a jogging outfit on and a hat. I never really saw her close up, only once or twice, but she always used to wave if she saw us as she came out of the alleyway.'

Norman produced a photo of Jenny. 'Is this her?'

The man studied it. 'Like I said, I never really saw her up close, so I couldn't be certain, but yes, I think that's her.'

'Can you recall what happened that day?' Norman asked.

'It was a Monday morning. It was unusual because there was a car stopped at the side of the road, back there a bit.' He pointed down the road. 'Me and the dog were about where you first saw us today, but I saw quite clearly what happened. Normally she jogs, you know, not too fast, but this particular morning, she came out of that alleyway like a bat out of hell, so fast she took the corner wide and ran out into the road.

'Then the car accelerated forward and hit her. I swear it was on purpose. It was as if he knew she was just about to come out of that alleyway, and he was waiting to run her down.'

'I don't suppose you got the registration number?' asked Norman.

'I'm sorry, no. I can tell you it was silver, a big four-wheel drive thing. But it all happened so fast, and to be honest, I was more concerned with what had happened to the woman.'

'Then what happened?'

'The car hit her so hard she went flying and ended up back on the pavement, right here by the lamppost, where we are now. Then another man came running from the alleyway, jumped into the car, and it sped off.'

'Could you describe the man?' Norman asked eagerly.

'I can tell you he was tall and slim, but that's about it. He didn't hang around long enough for a good look, and I was still quite a way off. I can tell you there was no attempt to see if she was alright. It was no accident.'

'What about the woman?' asked Darling.

'I rushed down here to help her,' he said. 'I covered her with my coat and told her to lie still while I went into my house to get some help. I live just there.' He pointed to a house across the road. 'I called for an ambulance and the police, and then I came back here, but she was gone by then.'

'Gone?'

'Yes, gone. I looked up and down the road here, then I ran up the alleyway into Derby Road in case she had got there somehow, but there was no sign of her.'

'How long were you in your house?' Darling asked.

'I was trying to be quick,' Hancock said, 'but I suppose it must have been three or four minutes.'

'Did you hear anything while you were in there? The car didn't come back for her?'

'I didn't hear anything, but then I would have been at the back of my house, so I wouldn't have heard a car coming back.'

'What did you do then?'

'I waited until the police and ambulance arrived and I had to explain that she had gone. They weren't too impressed that I'd called them out for nothing, I can tell you! It was quite embarrassing. I couldn't even prove I was telling the truth.'

'Well, thank you, Mr Hancock, you've been very helpful,' said Norman.

'Do you know if she's alright?' Hancock asked. 'Only we haven't set eyes on her since the accident.'

'She sustained a broken leg in the accident,' explained Norman. He didn't see the need to explain any further. 'So she's not going to be jogging any time soon.'

'Oh dear. Well, I'm not surprised she broke a leg. It's a wonder she wasn't killed.'

'She had a lucky escape,' Norman agreed.

'I hope you catch the people who did it,' said Hancock. 'Do you think you will?'

'We certainly intend to do our best, Mr Hancock,' said Norman determinedly.

———

'And so the plot thickens,' said Darling as she drove away.

'It certainly does,' said Norman thoughtfully.

'So what do you think? Was it a random event? An attempted robbery or something like that?'

'I don't really think so, do you? From what Hancock said, it sounded like it was planned. And anyway, what are you gonna rob from a jogger?'

'Do you think that car came back for Jenny while Mr Hancock was in his house?'

'Well, how far can a person run on a broken leg?' Norman asked. 'And her foot was smashed up too. The car coming back for her is the only thing that makes sense.'

'Are we talking about a kidnapping, then?' Darling asked.

Norman thought for a moment. 'If she was chased from that alley and then run down, I'm more inclined to think maybe it was a murder attempt that went wrong. Perhaps it was never meant to be a kidnapping, but they had to come back for her because she knew who they were.'

'You think it's the same tall guy from the pizza place?'

'It's a bit of a coincidence if it isn't, but it's also a pretty vague description. There must be plenty of tall, skinny guys in a town this size.'

Darling sighed. 'It's a pity we don't have a registration number for the car.'

'Yeah, knowing it's a silver, four-wheel drive doesn't help much, does it?'

'I know I'm not the boss here, Norm,' said Darling, 'but I don't think there's much doubt there's some sort of cover-up going on. I'm beginning to think we probably need some help, don't you?'

'The only way we might get any help is from Bradshaw, and I thought you said you didn't trust him.'

'Do you?'

'I dunno now,' Norman admitted. 'But I'm not sure how much further we can go on our own. I'm sure Casey's in this up to his neck, and if he is, how do we know he's the only one? That makes it risky going to the local police for help, so I have a feeling Bradshaw is our only option, whether we like it or not.'

CHAPTER THIRTEEN

Norman yawned as Darling pulled into a parking space at the motorway services. 'I'd forgotten how much I hate these clandestine early morning meetings,' he said as they walked into the main building and headed for the cafeteria.

'Norm, you hate early mornings full stop,' said Darling. 'It wouldn't matter if we were meeting Father Christmas, you'd still be moaning about it.'

'Yeah, well, I just don't see the need for anyone to get up at 6 a.m.'

'You didn't get up at 6 a.m.,' Darling said. 'It was well after six when I knocked on your door, and you were still in bed!'

'But I knew I had time to spare,' he argued.

'How come we only just got here in time then?'

'You were driving,' he said, indignantly. 'Perhaps if you had pressed a little harder with your right foot, we would have got here quicker.'

'Yeah, whatever. I can drive fast when the need arises, as you well know, but if you want us to collect speeding tickets, you can do it when you're driving. Anyway, where's this Bradshaw guy?'

Norman nodded towards the far corner of the room. 'He's over there in the corner, but he can wait a minute, I need coffee.'

'Good morning,' said Bradshaw, climbing to his feet when they

reached his table. He shook Norman's hand, then turned to Darling.
'And you must be Miss Darling. I'm very pleased to meet you.'

He shook her hand and pointed to a chair. When they were all
settled at the table, he looked at Norman. 'I assume you didn't ask me
here just to exchange pleasantries, so what can I do for you?'

'How about we go back to the beginning and you tell us all the stuff
you chose not to tell me before we started?'

'I'm not sure I know what you mean,' said Bradshaw.

'You know exactly what I mean. We're slowly uncovering something that stinks here, with at least one police officer covering things
up, so don't try to fob us off with any bullshit or we're going to start
thinking you're involved too!'

Now Bradshaw looked irritated. 'I'm not sure I like what you're
implying--'

'And I'm not sure I like being given half a story,' Norman
snapped.

'I think you may be getting bit above your station here, Norm.'

'So fire me.'

'Now, wait a minute--'

Norman pounded his fist on the table, making all the cups rattle
loudly. 'No, you wait a minute. You know a lot more about this case
than you're letting on, and if you want us to go any further, you're
going to have to tell us what it is. I think you knew all along that Jenny
had been murdered, and I've got a nasty feeling you might even know
who by.

'We've just discovered someone tried to run her down on a public
highway at around seven in the morning, when anyone could have been
on their way to work and seen them. If we're dealing with people
prepared to take risks like that, we wanna know what you know. That's
the deal – either you fill in some of the blanks, or we're out of here,
and you don't ever see us again!'

Bradshaw looked around the room, his face pink, but no one
seemed to be taking much notice of them.

Darling was impressed by Norman's speech, but not really
surprised. That was the thing about Norm; he tended to wear his heart
on his sleeve, and if you pissed him off, he wasn't shy about telling you.

She didn't know how Bradshaw might react, and she was intrigued to see what would happen next.

Bradshaw slowly raised his cup to his lips, all the while studying Norman's face. He sipped his coffee and placed the cup back on its saucer. Then he smiled appreciatively. 'I see having a heart attack hasn't diminished your fervour. You always were passionate about the truth, weren't you? And you're right. I did hold some information back, but I can see now that was a mistake. I hope you'll accept my apology. I should have told you everything.'

'Yeah, you should,' said Norman. 'But you can put that right here and now. It's not just for me. I asked Naomi to join me on this, but I didn't ask her to put her life at risk. Because you've kept stuff from me, you've made me mislead her. I'm not happy about that, and you should know it.'

Bradshaw nodded to acknowledge the truth of Norman's words. 'Miss Darling, I hope you'll accept my apology.'

'Sure I will, as long as you cut to the chase and fill us in on what we're missing,' she said.

'Of course. Where shall I start?'

'The beginning is usually a pretty good place,' Norman suggested.

Bradshaw clasped his hands in front of him. 'Now, let me get this right. You and Slater first met Jenny when you were investigating—'

'The Ruth Thornhill case,' finished Norman, impatiently. 'Yeah, yeah, we all know that bit. What we want to know is what's happened since then? Why she go off the rails? She never did tell us anything about that.'

'Not long after Ruth Thornhill, she was given the task of defending two men who had been accused of dealing drugs. It was a job no one in her firm wanted, but there was a lot of money at stake, so the senior partners took the job and handed it to their junior partner. They knew they would lose, but they were happy to sacrifice Jenny Radstock's reputation in order to make a fast buck. They figured she could be discredited and discarded afterwards, and they would survive any fallout and go on to live happily ever after. But they underestimated their junior partner.'

'She did her job, right?' Norman asked. 'She won the case?'

'Got it thrown out on a technicality and had half the drug squad reprimanded for unauthorised surveillance, harassment, and God knows what else.'

'And were these guys guilty?'

'Oh yes,' said Bradshaw. 'They had quite an organisation. It was drug money that paid for their defence. Everyone knew that.'

'So is it the police who've been making life difficult for Jenny?' asked Darling.

'Well, she certainly wasn't going to be voted their person of the year, but there was bit more to it than that. During the trial she got involved with one of the dealers.'

'Ah, jeez,' said Norman. 'I can see that wouldn't have been a good move.'

'It doesn't look good when someone who's supposed to be a pillar of the law is consorting with the worst sort of criminal,' Bradshaw agreed. 'It didn't take long for her to suffer the consequences of that decision, and when her own partners turned their backs on her, she became unemployable overnight. She lost her job and all that went with it.'

'That would have been one hell of a fall,' said Norman. 'But she was a smart cookie. Surely she could have got another job in some other field? Yet she was on the street when we found her.'

'You're right, she could have tried to get a job, but she didn't,' said Bradshaw. 'Instead, she moved in with her drug dealer boyfriend and lived off his ill-gotten gains.'

'You've known this all the time, haven't you?' asked Norman.

Bradshaw looked sheepish.

'You let Dave get involved with her, and all the time you knew what she'd been doing--'

'She'd split from her boyfriend before she met Slater,' said Bradshaw. 'That's why she was on the street. After he threw her out, she had nowhere to go. I didn't know she'd end up in Tinton with Slater!'

'But you said you were watching her, so you would have known where she was, and you could have told him,' Norman argued.

'What good would it have done? Besides, she needed someone to look out for her. I thought it might do both of them good. Anyway, all your arguing won't make any difference now, will it? She's dead!'

Part of Norman wanted to continue arguing with Bradshaw, but the realist in him knew there was no point. He wanted to see this job through, so he needed to cool down and ask some questions. 'Okay,' he said. 'So let's get some facts straight here. You say she left this drug dealer guy. Why did that happen? I would imagine she didn't want for anything with the sort of money a drug dealer tends to have.'

'I've got to be honest,' Bradshaw admitted, 'we're not exactly sure of all the facts concerning her relationship and why it ended. Surveillance was difficult because of the fallout after the court case.'

'So who are these guys?'

'They're brothers by the name of Ben and Jerry Shapiro. She had a relationship with Jerry.'

Darling was taking notes, but now she was suddenly fumbling for her pen as it nearly slipped from her fingers. 'Ben and Jerry?'

'Are they their real names?' asked Norman hastily.

'Yes,' said Bradshaw.

'D'you know where they are now?'

'Well, they were in London.'

'What's that supposed to mean?'

'It seems their operation is still active, but rumour has it there might be some sort of feud between the two of them. It's difficult to know for sure because of the surveillance situation, and they're not going to say, are they? They can't afford to let it be known they're at loggerheads. That would present a lot of their rivals with an opportunity to step in and take over.'

'Someone will be willing to spill the beans,' said Norman.

'That tends not to happen with these two. It appears anyone who has dared to speak against them in the past has disappeared very soon afterwards, never to be heard from again.'

'They sound like real charmers,' said Darling. 'What on earth did Jenny see in one of them?'

'Don't be too harsh,' Bradshaw said. 'We've all got involved with people we probably shouldn't have at some time. The head rarely wins where the heart's concerned.'

'I can't argue with that,' said Norman with a rueful smile, 'and I suspect Dave would agree too if he was here.' Then he added,anxiously, 'You're not going to get him here, are you?'

'No, definitely not,' said Bradshaw. 'I don't think he's ready for something as personal as this just yet.'

'Yeah, well, just make sure you keep him away.'

'Don't worry, I will.'

'What do these guys look like?' Norman asked.

'They're pretty unremarkable, really. Both six footers, both dark hair. I'll send you some photos later.'

'Either of them drive a big, silver four-wheel drive?'

'Not that I know of, but people like that change vehicles all the time. Why do you ask?'

'Someone suggested a vehicle like that could have been the one that ran Jenny down.'

'I can run some checks for you.'

'Yeah, that might be useful,' Norman said.

'Is that it now? Are we finished?' Bradshaw asked.

'No, I don't think we are yet. You seem to be deliberately avoiding something, and I want to know why.'

'I don't know what you mean.'

'Sure you do. When you first came to see me and Dave, you told us you were having Jenny watched for her protection.'

'Yes, that's right.'

'You told us some real bad people were after her. So who are these real bad people? Or was that just bullshit to lure us in?'

'My, my, you do have a low opinion of me, don't you?'

'So who are they?' Norman persisted.

'I think you might have got the wrong end of the stick. When I said we were watching her--'

'You said it was for her own protection because some bad people were chasing her,' Norman said. 'I have a great memory for these things, so don't try to feed me bullshit. Just tell me who these people are. You owe that to Naomi here, as well as to me.'

Norman was pretty sure he knew why Bradshaw had been watching Jenny back then, and he was quite enjoying watching him squirm. It was obvious the man was trapped between a rock and hard place.

'Are you going to tell Naomi the real reason you were watching Jenny, or shall I tell her?'

Bradshaw said nothing.

'I've got to be honest,' Norman said. 'I was willing to believe all the bollocks you told us about her being in hiding and how you were looking out for her, although I didn't totally buy the idea you could do that at the public's expense. But you made sure we didn't question what you said by offering Dave the chance to get back into his old job, so I didn't really pay too much attention back then.'

Darling had stopped writing long ago, and now she looked back and forth from Bradshaw to Norman, confusion written all over her face.

'But now I know what I didn't know back then,' Norman said. 'Now I know what Jenny never told us, and what you decided we didn't need to know. You weren't watching her for her protection, were you? You were watching her in the hope she would go back to her drug-dealing boyfriend and you would be able to follow her right there, weren't you?'

Darling's mouth dropped open, but Bradshaw's jaw tightened and his face hardened.

'Yeah, I thought so,' Norman said sneeringly. 'You didn't give a shit about her safety, did you? And I suppose that means we're considered expendable too, right?'

'Don't be so damned melodramatic,' said Bradshaw eventually. 'Yes, I admit we'd lost track of them, but it was her fault! If she hadn't pulled that case apart, those two would have been behind bars where they belonged.'

Norman stared at Bradshaw open-mouthed for a couple of seconds, and then his face broke into a broad grin. 'Wow! I just suddenly realised why this is such a touchy subject for you. It was your big drugs bust Jenny ruined, wasn't it?'

'I hate to disappoint you,' Bradshaw said, sniffing, 'but I've never worked for the drug squad, so there's no way I would have been involved in one of their cases.'

'So what's the score then?'

'Those men should have been put away for years, and instead of that, they walked away in an even better position than they were before. She ruined--'

'You can't blame Jenny for shortcomings in the prosecution's case,' said Norman. 'She just did her job better than you lot did yours. If the case had been put together right, she wouldn't have been able to pull it apart. You all underestimated her, didn't you? But then I bet you gave her no end of grief after. Was it your idea her firm should kick her out?'

'That was nothing to do with me,' said Bradshaw indignantly. 'It was her decision to shack up with a drug dealer that ended her career.'

'Then what happened? Did you ask her to sell him down the river? You expected her to do that to put the record straight, right? Can you imagine the danger you were putting her in?'

'I only arranged the surveillance on her,' Bradshaw said quickly. 'She wasn't supposed to be at risk. Yes, we were hoping she would lead us to him, but the plan was to get her out of the way and keep her safe. Anyway, it didn't matter in the end because she said no. Then, later, she seemed to have left Jerry and settled with Slater, so eventually the whole thing was called off.'

Darling went to speak, but Norman flashed her a look which made her think better of it. 'Is there anything else we need to know?' he asked Bradshaw.

'I don't think so.'

'You don't think so? Is that supposed to fill me with confidence?'

'Look, if you don't want to finish this job--'

'Oh, don't worry, we're more than happy to finish it,' said Norman. 'We just wanted to know we were being given a fair chance, that's all.'

'Alright,' said Bradshaw impatiently. 'I can assure you, you know everything I know.'

'Then we're done here,' Norman said. 'I can't think we have anything else to discuss with you. Come on, Naomi, let's get out of here.'

'I didn't realise you still hadn't told him about the letter,' said Darling as they walked to the car. 'You should have told me. I very nearly let the cat out of the bag.'

'Yeah, I'm sorry,' said Norman. 'You got my signal though, right?'

'You mean the face? I thought you were trying to turn me into a pillar of salt or something.'

'Aw, come on,' he said, putting an arm around her shoulders as they walked. 'It was just a look.'

'Oh, no, it was definitely a glare,' she said. 'It was the sort of look that could have made me burst into tears.'

'That's crap, and you know it. You're made of much tougher stuff than that. If I offended you that much, you'd probably punch me.'

'Don't tempt me,' she said, laughing.

CHAPTER FOURTEEN

'After our little chat with Mr Two-Faced Git Bradshaw, let me make sure I'm thinking what you're thinking,' said Darling as she drove them back onto the motorway. 'Let's start with Jenny. For reasons we don't yet fully understand, she's on the run and comes to Tinton. She finds you guys, makes eyes at Dave, draws him in, and then moves in with him.'

'You make that sound like she was looking for him all along,' Norman said.

'That's just how it seems to me. I told you I didn't like her because she was using him, and I think this proves I was right, don't you?'

Norman sighed. He didn't want to admit he was wrong about Jenny's motives towards Dave, but it was difficult to argue with her. 'Well, I don't think it's conclusive, but I'll concede it is possible you're right.'

'Alright! Result to me,' said Darling triumphantly. 'Anyway, where was I? Oh yeah, Jenny moves in with Dave. Now, we know Bradshaw has asked her to work for them, and we believe she's said no. But we also know Bradshaw underestimated her, so what if she's not dumb at all, and she realises they're still watching her and hoping? Maybe the reason she left wasn't because she split up with Jerry, but there was some other reason.'

'Like what?'

'I'm not sure yet, but just hear me out.'

'Okay, okay,' said Norman. 'I was just asking.'

'What if she left him because they both knew she was being watched? We know she can make it look like she's fallen out with someone. Maybe the plan all along was for her to stay out of the way until the heat died down and then to go back to him, unseen?'

Norman pulled an appreciative face. 'It's a bit out of left field, but that would work. But have you thought about how she might have sussed out she was being watched?'

'No, but you obviously have.'

'What if Bradshaw had actually approached her again? What if that's the bit he doesn't want to tell us?'

Darling nodded her agreement. 'D'you think that's what he's so cagey about the whole thing but still wants us to carry on? Maybe he feels it's all his fault she's dead.'

'It adds up, doesn't it?' agreed Norman. 'But carry on with your theory. I like what I've heard so far.'

'Well, that's about it, really,' she said. 'We already know she deliberately fell out with Dave so he wouldn't go looking for her.'

'So you agree she did care for him a little bit?'

'Yeah, okay, I'll perhaps give you that much, but that doesn't get away from the fact she used him. Anyway, I think she was going back to this Jerry guy, and, for whatever reason, she got stopped. God, you don't think Bradshaw had anything to do with that, do you? Let's be honest, he's got one hell of a motive if she ruined his rise to the top.'

'I'm beginning to think anything might be possible in this case,' said Norman gloomily, 'but we've already told him we think there's some sort of conspiracy going on. I think if he was that closely involved, he would have pulled us off it by now.'

'And you don't want to believe he's involved, do you?'

'No, I don't. I think he's guilty of making a complete mess of an operation, and he got her killed as a result, but I don't believe he would have <u>arranged</u> to have her killed. What would be the point?

What would he gain by it? If he suspected she was going back to the guy, surely he would have carried on watching her.'

Darling pulled a face. 'Yeah, I think you're probably right. Anyway, that's all I've got in the way of a theory. I thought it was pretty good while it was still in my head, but now it's out in the open, it doesn't really help much, does it?'

'If it's any consolation, I don't think I can add much to it,' said Norman. 'And there are some huge gaps, aren't there? If we're right to think she left Dave to come back to Jerry, what's she doing in Redville? Unless, of course, Jerry's also here somewhere.'

'He must be, mustn't he?'

'It's beginning to look that way, isn't it?'

'Finding him has to be our priority,' said Darling. 'It would help if Bradshaw gave us a photograph.'

'He said he'd send them, but I don't want to push it. We don't want Bradshaw to know we think Jerry's in town.'

'He'll be able to work that out for himself.'

'Probably,' Norman said. 'He might even already know exactly where he is, but let's hope he doesn't because we want to get to Jerry before he does, or we probably won't get the chance to talk to him.'

'I still don't understand why she had to end up dead,' said Darling. 'Who would have wanted her dead, and why?'

'In my experience, drug dealers don't have any sort of moral standards. I suppose if they did, they wouldn't do what they do. Bradshaw said they believe Ben and Jerry have fallen out and gone their separate ways. Maybe Jerry's here looking to set up an operation and the resident dealer wants to stop him. If that's the case, then it's just possible we've stumbled into a turf war, and Jenny's death was a means of getting at this guy Jerry.'

They fell into a gloomy silence for a few minutes until Norman spoke again. 'There is one thing you forgot to mention.'

'What's that?'

'You said you wanted to make sure you were thinking what I was thinking.'

'Yes, and?'

'You forgot to mention what I think of Bradshaw.'

Darling smiled. 'Ah, yes, but that's because I'm trying to give up using bad language. A young lady couldn't possibly use that sort of language.'

Norman went to open his mouth.

'Don't you dare say what you're thinking,' she warned him.

'What?' he said, innocently.

'You know what. You were going to say it would be alright for me to use that language because I'm not a young lady, weren't you?'

He smiled. 'Those weren't the exact words, but you've got the gist . . .'

CHAPTER FIFTEEN

It was grey and drizzly when they got back into town, so they headed for the church where Spiderhair had told them he got a free Friday lunch. They figured on a day like this it would be somewhere warm for him to shelter from the weather for an hour or so. He had previously mentioned the name Jerry, and Norman figured there was a distinct possibility he actually knew more about Jerry than he was letting on.

There were just a handful of people in the Church Hall when they peered in the door, but Spiderhair was nowhere to be seen.

'I guess I was asking a bit too much expecting him to be here just because I wanted to talk to him,' said Norman. 'Maybe we'll find him later.'

As he turned to walk away, he saw Jasper turning off the street and into the car park, heading for the church hall. He was walking with his head down against the weather, hands thrust deep into the pockets of his coat, but when he saw Norman, his face broke into a snarl, and he snapped upright. As he increased his stride towards them, he pulled his hands from his pockets, bunching them into fists, ready for action.

'Oh, crap,' muttered Norman. 'Looks like trouble heading our way.'

'I can handle him,' said Darling.

'No, hang on a minute. We don't want to keep humiliating the guy.'

'But he's just a bully.'

'Yeah, but even so. Let's see what's eating him first.' Norman put his hands forward, palms facing the fast-approaching Jasper. 'Whoa, now, Jasper, just hang on minute,' he said, standing his ground. 'You don't want to pick a fight with me. I had a heart attack not long ago. Too much hassle and I could drop dead. You don't wanna face a murder charge, do you?'

Jasper stopped just inches away from Norman, his chin jutting forward, fists at the ready. 'I ought to beat your head in,' he snarled.

'Just remember what happened last time,' warned Darling. 'I'd be quite happy to dump you on your arse again.'

Jasper looked down at her. 'You can do what you like, Missy,' he said. 'Make me look a fool if you will. I don't give a damn about me, but what you've done to young Spiderhair, now that ain't right.'

'What are you talking about?' Norman asked. 'We haven't done anything to him, apart from feed him and ask a few questions.'

'You took him somewhere. I want to know where you took him, and what the hell you did to him.'

'He found a mobile phone that belongs to someone we're looking for. He offered to show us where he found it if we drove him out there. So we took him to this street on the outskirts of town. Naomi offered to drive him back into town, but he said he wanted to walk back.'

'When was this?'

'Yesterday morning.'

Jasper stared uncertainly into Norman's face. 'You're lying. Tell me what you did to him!'

'I swear, he was fine when he left us,' said Norman, who was beginning to get a horrible feeling.

'Well, he ain't fine now, and as far as I'm concerned, it's all your fault.'

'What do you mean he's not fine now?' asked Darling, the concern clear in her voice. 'What's happened? Where is he?'

'You mean you really don't know?' Jasper asked, his voice a bit calmer.

'I promise you he was fine when we last saw him,' she insisted. 'Please tell me what's happened to him.'

'He didn't come back to camp last night, and I started to get worried, so I went looking for him. Poor little sod was in a terrible state when I found him. He was literally trying to crawl back to camp.'

'What happened to him?' Darling repeated.

'I don't really know. He couldn't speak properly. It looked as if he'd had some of his teeth knocked out.'

Darling's hand shot to her mouth. 'Oh my God. Who would do something like that?'

'I dunno,' said Jasper, 'but whoever it was wants to watch out, 'because if I find 'em--'

'Wait a minute,' said Norman indignantly. 'Are you saying you thought we had something to do with this?'

'Well, he was alright until you two came along and started asking questions. What am I supposed to think?'

'But we're investigators, not thugs!'

'Well you'd better get on and start investigating what's happened to the boy,' Jasper hissed into Norman's face, 'or you'll be investigating who buried an axe into the back of your head when you weren't looking!'

Norman recoiled at Jasper's garlic breath, but there was no mistaking the menace behind the threat. 'Look,' he said. 'We never intended the kid to come to any harm. If I'd thought anything like that would happen, I would never have gone anywhere near him.'

'He was doing fine until you came along. You turned his head,' said Jasper.

Norman felt quite helpless. Jasper obviously wasn't interested in listening to anything he might say.

'When you found him last night, did he say anything?' asked Darling.

'He was just making mumbling noises. Like I said, he seemed to have lost a few teeth. It was difficult to make out what he was saying.'

'Have you any idea?' Norman pleaded. 'Anything might help us, even if it doesn't seem to make sense right now.'

'He kept repeating the same thing. It might have been "men".

Yeah, now I think about it, he was probably trying to tell me some men had attacked him. I suppose that's not much help, though, is it?'

'Maybe, maybe not,' said Norman. 'We'll go to the hospital and see if we can speak to him right now. We'll do everything we can to find out who did this.'

———

By the time they got to the hospital, Norman had decided there was no point in messing around. There was only one way they were likely to find out where Spiderhair was, and playing it cool wasn't going to cut it. 'Just follow my lead,' he told Darling as they walked into the main reception area.

Norman marched right up to the harassed-looking woman behind the desk, who was talking to someone on the phone. Knowing she was distracted, he pulled the badge Bradshaw had provided from his pocket and flashed it quickly under her nose, making sure she didn't have time to study it before he put it back in his pocket.

'We're detectives Norman and Darling. We're investigating what we believe was the attempted murder of a young homeless guy who was brought in overnight. He had been pretty badly beaten up. Can you tell me where he is?'

The woman made a face at him, indicated the phone, and raised her eyebrows. It was obviously not the easiest call she'd had to deal with. Norman nodded and smiled his understanding. 'Just tell us which floor. We can take it from there.'

She put her hand over the mouthpiece. 'If it was last night, he'll be on the third floor. ICU's up there too.'

He gave her a hugely exaggerated thumbs-up. 'Got it,' he said. 'Thanks for your help.'

'You realise you could have just got her the sack?' asked Darling quietly as they headed for the lifts.

'She'll be fine,' said Norman as he pressed the button to call a lift. 'I doubt if anyone will even know we've been here.'

'Don't you think this is all a bit gung-ho? You've already got someone beaten up, and--'

'Hey, wait a minute. I seem to recall you were there, too, right? All we did was ask a few questions. Do you think I would have involved him if I had any idea this would happen?'

The lift arrived and they stepped inside. Darling looked distinctly sheepish as the doors swished closed. 'Well, no, I suppose not. I just feel so bad about this. Like Jasper said, he's just a kid.'

Norman turned to her, took her shoulders, and made her look at him. 'Look, I understand you feel bad about the kid, I do too, but we don't even know if this has got anything to do with us. Besides, blaming me, or yourself, isn't going to help him, is it? We need to find out who did this. The chances are it was just someone out to beat the crap out of some homeless kid simply because they could.'

Darling looked thoroughly miserable.

'C'mon, we can do this,' Norman said as the lift slowed to a halt.

The Intensive Care Unit was closest, so Norman headed there first. A nurse was sitting at a desk writing notes. 'You can see him,' she said, 'but you're not going to be able to speak to him. He won't be speaking to anyone, at least not for the time being.'

'We were told he was crawling when he was found last night,' said Norman.

'That's the survival instinct for you. It's nothing short of miraculous that he could do that.'

'He's that bad?'

'He's sustained multiple injuries, probably caused by a car accident.'

'He was hit by a car?'

'You don't really want me to go through it all again, do you?'

'Sorry?' Norman asked.

'No offence,' she said, 'but I am very busy. Your colleague is in with the patient now.'

Norman experienced a brief sinking feeling. 'Colleague?'

'I've already told him all of this, why don't you ask him?'

Norman was thinking fast. This could get decidedly awkward very quickly. 'Ah, yeah, right,' he heard himself saying. 'We'll do that.'

'Room three down on the right.' The nurse pointed down the corridor and then returned to her notes, the visitors soon forgotten.

Norman led the way down the corridor, stopped at the door, and peered through the window. 'It's Casey,' he said over his shoulder to Darling. 'What the hell's he doing here?'

'Well, if we can't talk to Spiderhair, maybe we should try him instead,' she suggested.

Casey couldn't hide his shock as Norman pushed the door open and led Darling into the room. 'You two? How the hell did you get in? What are you doing here?'

'I was going to ask you the same thing,' said Norman.

'I'm a police officer—'

'I've heard that rumour,' said Norman. 'But who's paying you to be here?'

'What's that supposed to mean?'

'Don't play the innocent with me. We know you're covering up what really happened to Jenny Radstock. I suppose the same person's paying you to make sure this kid can't talk.'

Casey snorted derisively. 'I don't know what you're talking about. He was hit by a car.'

'Just like Jenny,' said Darling. 'I'd say that's a bit of a coincidence, don't you agree?'

'There are lots of cars on the road.'

'And they're allowed to mow down pedestrians in this town, are they?'

'You've got no proof of anything,' said Casey. 'If we knew who was responsible—'

'Oh, I'm pretty sure you know who's responsible,' said Norman, 'But you'd better tell whoever it is that we're on to them, just like we're on to you, so they'd better watch out.'

'You're talking rubbish. You can't prove anything, and you know it. If I were you, I'd just go home and forget this case. You're in way over your head.'

'And you're in it up to your neck,' said Norman.

'You shouldn't be in here. I could have you arrested for this.'

'I think you'll find we'd be out in a couple of hours, and then all the attention's gonna turn on you. Go ahead, if that's what you want."

While the men were arguing, Darling had moved alongside Spider-hair's bed. She looked at the ghostly white face, the top of his head swathed in bandages. She took hold of his hand. It seemed ridiculously small on the end of his spindly, stick-thin arm. She gave his hand a squeeze, but the response she had hoped for just wasn't there. 'He's going to be so pissed off when he wakes up and finds his hair's been shaved off,' she said sadly.

Norman forgot Casey for a moment and stepped over to join her. He took in the machinery and stared at the assorted dials and screens. It all seemed calm enough, so he supposed that meant the boy was stable. It was scant consolation, but it was better than nothing.

There was a faint swooshing sound of a door closing, and he looked round to find Casey had gone. He thought about going after him, but decided it didn't really matter right now. They could deal with him later.

'This isn't right, Norm,' said Darling. 'I bet it's because of us. That's probably why Casey's sniffing around.'

Norman sighed. He had been thinking the same thing. He looked at Darling and noticed a single tear was slowly sliding down her cheek. She had been affected much more by this than he had realised. He used a finger to gently wipe the tear away.

'We don't know anything for sure, but you're probably right,' he told her. 'But you have to stop feeling guilty about it. If we're going to find out who did this, we need clear heads.'

'That's easy for you to say.'

He reached an arm round her and pulled her close. 'Yeah, I know, but that's one advantage of being so old, you see. I've had years of practice dealing with this stuff.'

Darling still had hold of the boy's hand.

'Come on,' said Norman, easing her away from the bed. 'Holding his hand isn't going to find who did this to him.'

CHAPTER SIXTEEN

They didn't even get close to the camp before Jasper came striding over to intercept them. 'Whadda you two want now?' he demanded. 'Haven't you caused enough trouble already? I've told the others they're not to speak to you, whatever inducement you might offer, so you might as well piss off. You're not welcome here.'

Norman raised his hands to indicate he hadn't come to fight with anyone. 'Look, I understand how you feel,' he said. 'Believe me, we feel really bad about what's happened to Spiderhair. Naomi here hasn't stopped crying. If we had had any idea this was going to happen, we would never have gone near him.'

'It's all your fault he's in that bloody hospital.'

'Yes, I know, I just admitted that, and you keeping on shouting at me isn't actually going to help him, is it?'

'If you think I'm going to tell you it's okay, and you don't need to worry--'

'I think I'm enough of a realist to know you're not going to forgive me anytime soon,' said Norman. 'Besides, nothing you can say is gonna stop me worrying about what's happened to the kid. But that's okay because I'm not looking for your forgiveness.'

'You're not?'

'I'm not going to forgive myself, so I'm hardly going to expect you to.'

Jasper eyed him suspiciously. 'So, what do you want?'

'I want you to help us.'

Jasper did a double take and then laughed out loud. After a few seconds, he stopped laughing and shook his head. 'I've got to hand it you, Mister, you've got some balls, but you've got some crazy bloody ideas too. Why would I want to help you, after what's just happened to Spiderhair?'

'Well, as the leader of this little group, I was hoping you'd wanna help find out who's responsible for what happened.'

'We already know who's responsible,' said Jasper. 'You are!'

Darling had been a silent bystander so far, but now she took a step towards Jasper, who retreated slightly. 'Fine, we admit we were the catalyst, but we didn't do the damage, did we?' she said. 'He was still in one piece the last time we saw him. It was someone else who tried to murder him.'

'But if you hadn't been poking your noses in where--'

'So you're saying whoever ran Spiderhair down should be allowed to get away with it, are you?' she snapped.

Jasper licked his lips and his eyes flicked between the two of them. 'There isn't anything the likes of us can do, is there?'

Norman had been watching Jasper's body language. 'You're looking uncomfortable, Jasper,' he said. 'I'm beginning to think you know who did it.'

'No, I don't,' he replied hurriedly.

'I think you do,' said Norman.

'Everyone knows there are certain things you can do in this town, and there are certain things you can't. Stay in line and you'll get by without too much hassle. Spiderhair stepped out of line, and he paid the price.'

'Who drew the line?'

'I don't know.'

'Or is it just that you're frightened to say?' asked Darling.

Jasper looked daggers at her. 'It's easy for you to stand there and judge,' he hissed. 'I bet when you leave here you'll go back to a nice warm bed in a nice safe home, won't you? You take that for granted, but people like us don't have that luxury. We have to huddle together to keep warm. We have to sleep out in the open where we're vulnerable to anyone who fancies kicking the shit out of us.'

Now it was Darling's turn to look uncomfortable.

'And I bet you've got plans, haven't you?' he continued. 'Something to aspire to and look forward to. Shall I tell you what I aspire to? Getting through the night and waking up in the morning, that's what. I wouldn't say I look forward to it, though. I mean, who in their right mind is going to look forward to a life like mine?'

There was an uncomfortable silence when he had finished speaking. Neither Darling nor Norman had been prepared for such an outburst, and they were both momentarily lost for words.

'Wow!' said Norman at last. 'Have you ever thought of going into politics?'

'Yeah, go on,' said Jasper. 'Take the piss, why don't you?'

'No, I'm serious. Anyone who can get their point across like that should be given a chance to do it.'

'Yeah, maybe so, but it's not going to happen, is it?'

'But if someone's put the fear of God into you all, don't you think they should be stopped?' asked Darling. 'Don't you want to fight back?'

'What chance have we got?' Jasper gave a hollow laugh. 'Don't forget, we're at the bottom of the food chain. We'll just end up like Spiderhair. What good will that do?'

'You might be at the bottom, but we're not,' Norman said. 'If you help us, we can help you.'

'We've seen what your help does.'

'Look, I get what you're saying, but we can bring in additional resources,' said Norman.

Jasper snorted loudly. 'What, like the local police? They're part of the problem!'

'Yeah, we already know that, but we're not that sort of police, and we're not local.'

'It's too big,' said Jasper. 'They've got everything tied up around here.'

'Who are they?' asked Darling.

'That's just it. No one actually knows who's behind it. I think it's all to do with drugs, but I can't prove it.'

'Why do you think that?' asked Norman.

'Coastal town, easy access to France across the channel. I've been down the harbour when some of them boats come in. They're supposed to be sailing yachts, for pleasure, you know? More like drug carriers if you ask me. I reckon there's shedloads coming in all the time, but half the local police are on the take, and customs are the same.'

'Did you ever meet a girl called Ginger?' asked Norman. 'Well, I say girl, she was actually in her late thirties. Nice-looking, black hair.'

'Yeah, I met her once or twice. It was Spiderhair who really knew her.'

'He said she was like a big sister to him,' said Darling.

'Yeah, that's right. She used to look out for him. She died from an overdose, didn't she?'

'That's the official story,' said Norman. 'We think that's bullshit, and we're here to find out what really happened to her. That's why we were talking to the kid.

'Let me guess.' Jasper motioned like he was sticking a syringe into his arm. 'Syringe in the arm, enough heroin to kill an elephant.'

'Got it in one,' said Norman suspiciously. 'But now I can't help wondering how come you knew that and Spiderhair didn't.'

'I knew he'd be upset, so I kept it to myself.'

Norman studied Jasper's face. He was sure the man was lying, but he also knew how to hide it.

'She must have been dealing,' Jasper continued, 'or owed them a lot of money for them to do that to her. It's their favourite way of letting everyone else know it's best not to cross them.'

'Who? asked Darling. 'Who is it best not to cross?'

'Whoever's controlling the drug supply, of course.'

'Yes, but who is it? You've got your ear to the ground. Surely you must know.'

'And how would I know that, exactly?' asked Jasper. 'Do I look like I can afford to buy drugs? That's one thing I've always steered clear of, even when I had money.'

'Have you ever heard of someone called Jerry?' Norman asked.

Jasper grinned. 'Doesn't he get chased by Tom?'

'You want to be careful,' said Norman drily. 'You're that sharp, you might cut yourself.'

Jasper ignored the sarcasm. 'Should I have heard of him?'

'Spiderhair mentioned him. He said he thought Ginger might have been staying with him. I was hoping you might know where we could find him.'

'Sorry, I can't help you there.'

'Okay, no problem,' said Norman. 'It was a long shot. Thanks for talking to us, you've been really helpful.'

'But I said I wasn't going to help you.'

'Ah, but you did, though, and we appreciate it.'

'Hang on a minute,' began Jasper. 'I'm not bloody helping you for nothing.'

Norman gave him a wicked grin. 'Sorry, can't stop.' He stuck his hands deep into his pockets. 'Crap! I'm clean out of cash too. I'll drop by tomorrow. You stay safe now.'

He ushered Darling back to the safety of the open street.

'You sure know how to take advantage of people and piss them off, don't you?' she said. 'He's not going to help us tomorrow after that.'

'Oh, he's going to help us,' said Norman. 'I guarantee it. I'm just not sure if it'll be tomorrow or later tonight.'

'You've lost me.'

'Unless I'm very much mistaken, our new friend Jasper is going to be making contact with the very person he claims not to know. And once he's mentioned the conversation we've just had, I expect someone to come looking for us.'

'You think?' asked Darling. 'But why would he tell us about the drug shipments if he's working for them?'

'I don't suppose he's telling us anything that isn't common knowl-edge locally anyway. You hear the same story in any town by the sea. I have to admit, he's pretty good at playing his part. I hope they pay him well.'

'And you're quite sure about this are you? Because he convinced me.'

'That's because you were only looking at his eyes,' said Norman.

'The window to his soul,' she said.

'That's as maybe, but you have to remember – windows can be dressed.'

'That's bit vague, Norm. You'll have to do better than that.'

'Doesn't it strike you as being a bit odd that a homeless guy can manage to keep himself clean-shaven all the time? We've seen him two or three times now, and there's never been a trace of stubble on his face.' He rubbed a hand over his own chin. 'Now, I'm not one of those guys who can grow a beard in five minutes, but even I have stubble by the end of the day.'

'Some guys just don't grow a beard,' Darling said unconvincingly.

'And what about his shoes?'

'What about his shoes?'

'They're too clean,' said Norman. 'And his clothes look as though they're freshly laundered. The only dirty thing about him is that shabby old coat. Remember Spiderhair said he disappears for hours at a time during the day? I reckon it's because he's got a pad somewhere and he goes home to shower, shave, change his clothes, and catch up on some sleep.'

'Don't you think the others would have noticed by now?'

'How many of them are looking? He offers them some sort of security at night, so they only see what they want to see. He's also hiding behind that shabby old coat, and he's made sure most of them are scared to challenge him, right?'

'There's no need to be quite so smug about it,' Darling said irritably. 'Overconfidence can be a terrible turn-off for a girl.'

'Yeah, so I've been told,' Norman said good-naturedly, 'but as I'm not trying to turn you on, I don't see it's an issue. Besides which, I know I'm right, so overconfidence doesn't come into it.'

CHAPTER SEVENTEEN

'Where exactly are we supposed to be going?' asked Darling next morning as she walked slowly alongside Norman. 'We've been walking round and round in circles for half an hour now. It wouldn't be so bad, but you won't even let me go into any of the shops!'

'We're not going anywhere in particular,' said Norman, 'and we're not going into any shops. We're waiting for someone to come and find us.'

'Any particular someone?'

'I dunno. But it occurred to me that this Jerry guy might be trying to set up his own operation, and having eyes on the ground would be more than useful.'

'And you actually think he's going to come and find us?'

'Not in person. If he's a major player like Bradshaw says, and I'm right about him moving into someone else's territory, he's not going to risk showing his face. People like that tend to keep a low profile. He'll have guys working for him.'

'So we get to start our day the hijacked way. That's just terrific!' said Darling, her voice dripping with sarcasm. 'Am I getting paid danger money? I expect at least double time if someone's going to be pointing a gun at me.'

'Look, this is Redville-on-Sea, not Chicago in the prohibition era,' said Norman. 'No one is going to want to draw attention to themselves by pointing a gun at you in a place like this. How about I pay you extra if you stop complaining?'

'Maybe if you kept me better informed, I wouldn't have anything to complain about.'

Norman sighed, stopped walking, and turned to face her. They were standing by the kerbside. 'I'm sorry. You're right, I need to communicate a bit more.'

'No,' said Darling, 'you don't need to communicate a bit more. You need to communicate a lot more. It's not as if you keep notes I can refer to. You keep everything in your head, and you only share odd bits when it suits you. I understand you're the boss, but it does help if I have some idea what your plans are. Is this how you work with Dave?'

'Err, no,' he admitted guiltily. 'I tend to let him take the lead. He's much better organised than me.'

Darling rolled her eyes. 'Well, now, there's a surprise.'

'He's pretty good at making sure we both know what's going on too.'

'Ah! So you do know what communication is, you're just no good at doing it.'

'Look, I said I'm sorry. How bad do you want to make me feel?'

'Bad enough for you to change your ways would be quite good.'

Before Norman could reply a large blue Mercedes pulled up alongside them. As they turned to look, the passenger window glided silently down, and the driver leaned across. He was the sort of guy who could have been described as hired muscle, but there didn't seem to be any menace about him.

'Are you Norman?'

'Yeah, that's me. Why, who's asking?'

'Jerry wants a word.'

'Are you Jerry?' Norman asked.

'What do you think?'

'I think it's unlikely.'

'Are you going to get in?'

'If I don't?'

'Then I drive away and you miss the opportunity to talk to him.'

'Isn't this where you pull a gun and threaten to blow our heads off?' asked Norman. He wiggled a thumb at Darling. 'Only Naomi here was expecting a team of guys hanging out of the windows waving machine guns.'

'Maybe in a previous life,' said the driver, 'but not these days. Do you want to speak to Jerry, or do I leave you here? It's your choice.'

'Well, you can count me in,' said Darling. She stepped forward, opened the back door, and climbed in. 'I don't know about him, though,' she said as she slid across the seat. 'He has a problem sharing his thoughts.'

The driver looked confused.

'Take no notice,' said Norman as he climbed into the car. 'She seems to have got out of bed on the wrong side this morning.'

The driver took a look at the two of them in his mirror, put the car into gear, and eased away from the kerb. 'So it's Norman and Naomi,' he said. 'It's got a nice ring to it. I'm Dennis, by the way.'

'I have to say, this isn't quite how I thought this would work,' said Norman.

'What, you were expecting machine guns too?'

'Not guns exactly. I figured that would be a bit out of place in a town like this. I thought maybe two or three guys and a lot more threatening language, like you see in the movies.'

Dennis laughed. 'Sorry to disappoint you, but I meant it when I said you didn't have to get in the car. Jerry would be disappointed because he wants to talk to you, but he's not about to force you to come if you don't want to. You can still change your mind and get out if you want.'

Darling looked at Norman and raised her eyebrows. He was just as surprised. This wasn't at all what he was expecting. 'No, it's okay, Dennis,' he said. 'I think you've created enough intrigue that we just have to see this through now.'

'Oh, good. Jerry will be pleased.'

CHAPTER EIGHTEEN

They had driven about a mile out of town when the Mercedes slowed and then turned left off the road. 'Is this it?' asked Norman.

'Just up the drive here,' said Dennis. 'Jerry asked me to take you to the gazebo.'

'Did you say gazebo?' asked Darling.

'He likes his garden, does Jerry. The weather's a bit shit for sitting out this time of year, but he can still enjoy it if he uses the gazebo.'

'What's he like? Is there anything we should know?'

'He's not everyone's cup of tea, but I like him,' said Dennis. 'He looks after me, and I look after him, but even though I work for him, he never looks down on me, you know? Just be straight with him and you'll be fine.'

'You make him sound like an all-round nice guy,' said Norman.

'Yeah, well, that's because he is.'

'That's quite an unusual quality for a drug dealer.'

Dennis pulled a face. 'But he's not a drug dealer.'

'That's not what I heard,' said Norman.

'Maybe you've been talking to the wrong people,' said Dennis, bringing the car to a stop. 'This is where you get out.'

'Did I say something wrong?' asked Norman doubtfully.

'No, don't worry, you're fine. I'm not throwing you out. You have to walk the last bit to the gazebo.' Dennis pointed to a group of trees about fifty yards away. 'Follow the path down to those trees. The gazebo's just behind them. You'll see it when you get down there. When you want to go home, just come back here, and I'll be waiting.'

Norman wasn't convinced this wasn't some sort of trap. He looked at the trees and back at Dennis.

'You don't trust me, do you, Norman?' asked Dennis.

'I'll admit I'm not exactly one hundred per cent happy with this situation.'

Dennis turned to Darling. 'Have I done anything to suggest you're in any danger since I picked you up?'

'No, you haven't. Come on, Norm. We've come this far. We might as well see it through.'

Before Norman could react, she had opened the door and stepped out. 'Hey wait,' he called after her as he scrabbled to open his own door. 'Don't rush off on your own. Wait for me.'

She was halfway to the trees before he caught up with her. 'I thought you were the one who was worried about what could happen.'

'Yeah, well, we're here now, aren't we?' she said. 'And like you said, Dennis the driver has made this Jerry sound so intriguing, we've got to see what we've been missing, haven't we?'

'I was worried about you! I thought you were scared.'

'Oh, come on, Norm. I'm an adrenaline junkie. I can't help it.'

'False bravado can get you into a lot of trouble,' he warned.

'It's not bravado, and it's not false,' she said. 'I just don't scare easily. Ask yourself – when have you ever seen me really scared of anything?'

'What about the rat?'

'Alright, apart from rats.'

'Well, now you come to mention it . . .'

'Exactly. I just don't feel it like other people do.'

They had reached the trees now, and they could make out a rather magnificent gazebo just beyond. They followed the path through the trees. 'There it is,' said Darling as it came fully into view. 'Wow! Look at it.'

'Jeez, that's as big as a house,' said Norman.

The path led up to a door that was ajar. Norman knocked and pushed the door, which swung open to reveal a small hallway. He led Darling inside and pushed the door closed behind them, leaving the chilly autumn air outside.

An inner door opened to reveal a man Norman guessed to be about forty years old. He was about six feet tall, with long, straggly hair and an untidy beard. He looked as if he hadn't slept recently. 'Hi,' he said. 'You must be Norman, and you're Naomi, is that right?'

'Yes, that's right,' she said.

'I'm Jerry. Why don't you come on in?'

Norman looked at Darling, who gave an almost imperceptible shrug. This whole situation was so unlike what he had been expecting, he was still struggling to come to terms with it, and he really wasn't sure. There again, they'd come this far . . .

He looked at her again, and this time he was sure she nodded. He looked at Jerry, who smiled encouragingly. 'Yeah, sure, why not?'

He ushered Darling through the door, following closely behind her.

'I've got coffee, or would you prefer tea?' asked Jerry as he led them into the main part of the gazebo. He pointed to a dining table and some chairs set out in front of a huge window that gave a view across the garden and on for miles beyond.

'Wow!' said Norman. 'This is quite a place. And this is just the gazebo? I could happily live in a place this size.'

'It's pretty cool, isn't it?' asked Jerry. 'I'm renting this place at the moment. I'd quite like to buy it, but it's not really where I want to settle.'

His eyes seemed to suddenly glaze over, and for a moment, Norman thought he was going into some sort of trance, but then he seemed to shake himself out of it. 'Mind you,' he said gloomily, 'everything's changed now, so I don't know what I'm going to do.'

He seemed to be about to drift off again, but Norman wasn't having any of that. 'The message we got was that you wanted to talk to us.'

'What? Oh, yeah, that's right,' said Jerry, dragging himself back into the real world. 'A little birdie tells me you've been looking into what happened to Jenny.'

'That little birdie wouldn't be called Jasper, by any chance, would he?'

A smile flitted across Jerry's face. 'He said he thought you'd probably made him,' he said. 'It helps to have ears on the ground, you know? My brother taught me that.'

'But why would you need to have ears anywhere?' asked Norman.

'Right now I seem to have a lot of enemies, and when that happens, it's usually a good idea to keep track of what's going down and when.'

'How d'you come to make so many enemies?' asked Darling.

Jerry gave them an indulgent smile. 'Sorry, but that isn't how this is going to work. I didn't ask you out here so you could question me. You're here so I can ask the questions, and you can give the answers.'

'Maybe we need to ask you some questions to help us work out all the answers,' said Norman.

Jerry nodded once. 'Perhaps,' he said. 'But you answer my question first. Are you investigating what happened to Jenny?'

'You didn't know her as Ginger, then?'

'That was her street name, we all know that, so let's stop playing games.'

'Yeah, we are investigating,' Norman said, 'but what's it to you?'

Jerry's eyes flashed angrily. 'She was everything to me,' he snapped. 'We were going abroad to start a new life together, but someone murdered her before that could happen. I want to know who it was.'

'You think she was murdered?'

'She was found with a syringe in her arm, but she never, ever touched drugs. She wouldn't even smoke a little dope.'

'We kinda worked that one out too,' Norman said. 'We also guessed you were the reason she was here, and I'm really sorry you've lost her, but we can't tell you who did it because we don't know. And even if we did know, we couldn't tell you. You must know that.'

'I can pay. You'd never have to work again.'

Norman sighed. 'Yeah, but you see, it's not about the money. Even if it was, that would mean accepting bad money, and I'm not even vaguely interested in doing that.'

'What do you mean, bad money? My money's as good as anyone's.'

'We have little birdies that talk to us too,' said Norman. 'They're not the same ones you talk to, but I reckon ours are probably better informed. Anyway, one of our little birdies told us you deal drugs, and that means your money is drug money. Like I said, that's bad money.'

'I'm not involved in that any more. I promised Jenny I'd leave that life behind me and we would start again.'

'Well it's always good to hear someone's changing their life for the better,' said Norman, 'but I expect you're doing it with a nice healthy bank balance, right?'

'Well, yes, of course.'

Norman shook his head and tutted. 'And that bank balance was created by selling drugs, right? It doesn't matter which way you look at it, that's not really starting again, is it?'

'What gives you the right to judge me?' Jerry asked angrily.

'Hey, I'm not judging you. I just have a different moral code, and what you do doesn't fit with my code. That's just how it is. If you can do what you do and live with yourself, well, good for you, but I don't want any part of it, and that especially includes your money.'

'Well, at least tell me what you know.' Jerry was pleading now. 'I can't even find out what really happened to her. The police won't tell me anything.'

Norman looked at Darling. 'Well, I suppose at least now we know it's not Jerry here who's paying Sergeant Casey to keep his mouth shut.'

'That explains why he wouldn't take my money,' said Jerry.

'Yeah, someone's beaten you to it,' said Norman, 'and whoever it is, I reckon they must be paying him top money. So who around here would be able to do that?'

'I don't know anyone here,' said Jerry. 'The only reason I came here was to meet Jenny. We were going to stay here for a couple of weeks while we made our plans, and then we were going to run away.'

'Run away?' asked Darling. 'Why would you need to run away? Who are you running from?'

'It's just a figure of speech,' said Jerry hastily. 'We were going to get new passports and new IDs, set up somewhere abroad, and never come back.'

'Look,' said Norman. 'I wouldn't take your money if it was the only thing that would keep me alive, but I do want to find out what happened to Jenny. I don't know if she ever told you, but I knew her, and she spent a lot of time living with a friend of mine, so this case is a bit personal to me.'

Something seemed to click in Jerry's mind. 'You mean that Dave Slater guy? Yeah, Jenny told me about him. You must be Norman Norman, right? I should have put two and two together when Jasper told me your name.'

'One of the reasons we're here is so we can tell Dave Slater what happened to Jenny. I think after he looked after her for so long, you owe him that much, don't you?'

He was surprised to see Jerry looked guilty.

'Naomi has always had this theory that Jenny was using Dave. I didn't think she was right at first, but now I think she's got it spot on. Jenny was waiting for you to get in touch with her, wasn't she? So how about you tell us why she had to hide? It might just help us figure out who's behind what happened here.'

Jerry didn't look convinced, and for a few moments, Norman thought that was going to be the end of the conversation, but then he relented. 'Okay, how far back do I need to go? I take it you know about the court case?'

'That's where you met her, right?'

'Yeah. I knew from the first moment I set eyes on her that she was special, and we hit it off straight away, but being in the business I was in, it was never going to be easy, was it?'

'You mean drug dealing? You're right, it's not exactly the best career for the boyfriend of a barrister.'

'Let's get something straight, can we?' Jerry said firmly. 'It's my brother, Ben, who's the drug dealer, not me. I'm just an accountant.'

'Specialising in creative accountancy on your brother's behalf, no doubt.'

'I didn't ask where the money came from, right? I just kept the books.'

'And because you kept your eyes averted, that made it alright, did it?' asked Darling.

'D'you want to hear this or not?'

'Yeah, we do,' said Norman, 'but can you stop playing the innocent? You might not have actually handled any drugs yourself, but you knew exactly what was going on, and you were happy enough to take the money.'

It was clear from their faces that Norman and Darling weren't about to change their opinions. After a few moments, Jerry continued his story.

'Shortly after the case ended, Jenny's mother died, and with no one to look after her father, she had to put him into a nursing home. He has Alzheimer's, you see, and he needed constant attention. She stopped going to see him in the end because he had no idea who she was. She hated herself for it, but she just couldn't deal with seeing him like that.'

Norman's brow creased. 'She never told us about any of that. How do we know this is all true.'

'You're detectives, aren't you?' said Jerry mockingly. 'It can't be that difficult to check it out if you don't believe me. It seems there are a lot of things she didn't tell you. She didn't tell you about me, did she? Some people share everything, and some people keep it inside. She preferred to keep it inside. It's how she dealt with stuff.'

It was becoming increasingly clear to Norman he hadn't actually known Jenny at all, so he didn't feel he could argue the point any further.

'Anyway, like I said, we just seemed to hit it off, and when all the family stuff happened, I think she needed someone to lean on, and I was there. It was a case of right time, right place, as it were. Within a matter of weeks, she'd moved in with me.'

'How did Ben feel about that?'

'He was fine about it. Why wouldn't he be? It didn't make any difference to what he was doing.'

'He didn't think her being part of the legal system might be a problem?' Norman asked carefully.

'But she wasn't part of it any more, was she? She left all that behind to come and live with me.'

'It could be argued that getting involved with you destroyed her career, and that coming to live with you was the only option she had left.'

'Yes, you could argue that was the case, but it wasn't like that. The loss of her mother and the situation with her father had turned her life upside down. Maybe that's what drove her decision, but whatever it was, she chose me over them.' Jerry stared at Norman, daring him to argue.

'Whatever,' said Norman, unconvinced. 'So what then?'

'It was good for a few weeks. She started to get over her problems, and we were really happy, and then things started to happen. First of all, we started getting threatening letters saying Jenny was going to be a target.'

'Who from?'

'We had no idea at the time, but it got even worse. I expect you know Jenny likes to keep herself fit?'

Norman nodded.

'She used to go jogging for half an hour or so every morning. One day, someone jumped out of a car and tried to grab her.'

'Did she see who it was? Or recognise the car?'

'She managed to slip away, but she was so scared she couldn't even remember the colour of the car. She stopped jogging after that. I offered to get her a bodyguard to go jogging with her, but she was adamant there was just no way. She didn't run again until she was with Slater.'

'So how did she end up on the street?'

'I'm just getting to that,' Jerry said. 'The threats against her started to increase. There were phone calls, letters, you name it, we got it. Ben was getting them too. When a couple of our guys lower down the food chain got bumped off, Ben thought it was the beginning of a turf war and a rival gang was trying to scare us off. They obviously didn't know Ben very well.'

'Tough guy, huh?' asked Norman.

'He's not someone you threaten unless you're prepared to carry the threat out and suffer the consequences. I know he's my brother, but Ben's not someone you want to mess with. He's the sort of guy who would start a war if someone looked at him the wrong way.'

'So you thought whoever was making the threats must be serious,' Darling suggested.

'Or incredibly stupid,' Jerry said. 'Anyway, I wasn't prepared to put Jenny's life at risk, so we came up with a plan whereby she would go underground, and I would let people think we'd had a bust-up and I'd thrown her out.'

'Who's "we"?' asked Norman. 'You said "we" came up with a plan.'

'Well, it was actually her idea. I think it might even have been a way of punishing herself for putting her father in a home.'

'And you went along with letting her live on the street?' asked Darling. 'Do you know how much danger a woman living on the street has to face?'

'Of course I knew the risks,' snapped Jerry. 'But she insisted, and if there was going to be a turf war, I couldn't guarantee she would be safe with me. It was the last place anyone would look for her, and she was pretty sure she could find this Dave Slater guy. And if she did find him, she thought he would look out for her. And she was right. He did.'

Norman sighed and exchanged a look with Darling, who pulled an 'I told you so' face, but there was no satisfaction in her voice when she spoke. 'Didn't I tell you she was just using him?'

'That was something she just had to do,' said Jerry.

'No, she didn't have to do it the way she did,' said Norman. 'She pretended to rekindle an old fling and used his feelings for her own ends. She chose to deceive a man who would have offered her shelter as a friend if she had just asked. There was no need for her to do that.'

Jerry looked suitably sheepish.

'Were you in touch with her while she was with him? You were, weren't you?'

'She had her own mobile phone, and a pay-as-you-go one so no one could trace it.'

'So you knew what she was doing all the time. In that case, I assume you knew she was going to lead him on and bed him?'

'And you were okay with that?' asked Darling before Jerry could speak.

'It was necessary!'

'I just told you it wasn't,' said Norman. 'Don't you people have any morals at all?'

Jerry's face flushed. 'Look,' he snapped. 'I know you think it's wrong, but it's happened now, and she's dead anyway. Debating the rights and wrongs isn't going to tell us who killed her, is it?'

'I suppose you're right about that,' said Norman wearily. 'So who else knew about this master plan of hers?'

'Just Jenny and me,' said Jerry.

'You didn't tell Ben?'

'I didn't see the need. I thought the fewer people who knew, the less risk there was.'

'Did it ever occur to you that Jenny could have been deceiving you, just like she deceived Dave?' asked Darling. 'She was very good at deception, wasn't she?'

'Why would she have been deceiving me?'

'Well, maybe she wasn't quite as happy about losing her career as you thought. Maybe her plan was to get into your organisation so she could inform on you.'

Jerry sighed impatiently. 'If you're talking about that Bradshaw guy asking her to set me and Ben up, she told me about that. He had asked her after the case, then when she first came to live with me, and he asked her again when she started living with Slater. I think if she'd been out to get us, we'd be locked up by now, don't you?'

'There's no need to get uptight,' said Norman. 'We're just exploring theories here. Someone must have had a reason for wanting her dead. We're just trying to figure out who that might have been. You know she was hit by a car, right?'

Jerry stared at him. 'What?'

'She was hit by a silver car when she was out jogging. That's how she came to lose her mobile phone, and that's how a kid called Spider-hair came to find it. A guy who lived near the accident ran into his house to phone for help, but by the time he got back, she had gone. We think whoever ran her down must have gone back for her.'

For the first time, Jerry looked genuinely upset. 'Jesus, so that's how she came to end up in that filthy squat. Did you have to tell me that?'

'I thought you asked us to tell you what happened.'

'Yes, but . . . well, I suppose we know who did it then. There's only one option, isn't there?'

'Is there?'

'It must be the same people who tried to abduct her before.'

'Oh, I see what you mean,' said Norman. 'But that doesn't help if we don't know who they are, does it?'

'It shouldn't be that hard to identify them.'

'Did you identify them before?' asked Darling

'Err, well, no.'

'Really?' said Norman. 'All those people on the ground, and you had no idea?'

'What are you saying?' Jerry demanded.

'I'm not saying anything,' said Norman innocently. 'I'm just thinking if you guys couldn't find out who it was, what chance have we got?'

'So what are you going to do?' Jerry asked.

'We're gonna go back into town and keep asking questions.'

'You'll tell me what you find?'

'I doubt it,' said Norman. 'You've got plenty of money. Why don't you find yourself a detective to search for you? Come on, Naomi, let's go. We've got a long walk ahead of us.'

'Dennis will drive you back into town.'

'Don't think that will make any difference.'

'I don't,' said Jerry. 'But when he brought you up here, Dennis told you he'd take you back. That was the deal. I like to keep a deal.'

CHAPTER NINETEEN

They barely spoke as Dennis drove them back into town, and once back, they decided to stop for lunch. When they were settled at their table, waiting to be served, Norman voiced his thoughts. 'Here's the thing. According to Bradshaw, the Shapiro brothers have a huge drug operation, right?'

'Yes, except Jerry seems to think he's no longer part of it.'

'Whether he's still part of it is neither here nor there, so ignore that for a minute. My point is, whoever runs a drug operation that big must have a small army of people on the ground, and enough money to buy just about any information they want. And yet Jerry says they couldn't identify the guy who tried to abduct Jenny, or the competitor they thought might be trying to muscle in on their territory. Does that sound likely to you?'

'Yeah, I see what you mean,' Darling said thoughtfully. 'D'you think he was lying?'

'Isn't it good business to know who your competitors are and what they're up to? It must be even more important when it comes to heavy stuff like drug dealing. You don't stay on top in that world without knowing who's who and what's what.'

'But if they knew who it was, they would have done something about it, wouldn't they?'

'Well, yeah, you would think so,' Norman said. 'But maybe we're looking at it the wrong way. What if Jerry's telling the truth, and as far as he knows, they didn't find out who was responsible?'

'I don't want to appear thick,' Darling said, screwing her face up, 'but I think you might be in danger of losing me here.'

'Well, think about what we know,' said Norman. 'Jerry says Ben didn't have a problem with him having a relationship with Jenny. Consider that for a minute. Two brothers have been partners in a huge illegal business for a few years, making shedloads of money, and now one of them has decided to bring a girlfriend into their world. If you were Ben, would you be happy about that?'

'They are brothers,' Darling reminded him.

'Yeah, but don't forget – the girlfriend in question just happens to be a woman who's spent half her life working in the legal establishment. Bradshaw mentioned a possible feud, and we know Ben's not exactly the warm, cosy, user-friendly sort of drug dealer, is he?'

Darling's eyes widened. 'You think Ben sent threats to his own brother's girlfriend?'

'Is it so unthinkable? Remember what I said earlier – these people have different morals. What if Ben didn't trust Jenny? Okay, she might have saved his arse from a prison sentence, but that doesn't mean he's happy for her to come along and be part of the family business. He must have been aware of the outcry when Jenny won their case, but maybe he doesn't buy this idea she's been forced to quit the legal profession. What if he thought she could be part of an elaborate plan to finally put them behind bars?'

'So there never was a competitor trying to move in?'

Norman shook his head. 'If Ben had tried to persuade Jerry to get rid of Jenny, his feelings about her would have been obvious. By suggesting there was a turf war brewing, and then arranging for someone else to send the threats, he could put Jerry off the scent. Don't forget, Jerry doesn't get his hands dirty, so it figures he would only know what Ben told him about what goes down on the street.'

'So you think Ben was behind all the threats, and Jerry had no idea?'

'That's my thinking.'

'That means he even tried to have her kidnapped!' Darling whistled.

'And quite possibly he's behind her death.'

'But can you be sure Jerry didn't know? Don't forget, he kept the plan for Jenny to go into hiding from Ben, didn't he? Maybe that's why he was planning to leave.'

'I can't deny it's a possibility,' said Norman.

'Maybe Jerry thought he could escape without Ben finding out.'

'Yeah, you could be right. But imagine how Ben would feel about that if he did find out? He thought he'd got rid of the problem of having Jenny around the place only to find she's back on the scene and Jerry's sneaked off to join her, and this time she's going to take his brother away.'

'It all adds up, doesn't it?' Darling said slowly. 'He's got the motive, the means, and once she's surfaced here with Jerry, waiting to leave, he's got the opportunity. Are you going to tell Jerry about this?'

'I'm not going to tell anyone,' said Norman. 'Right now it's only a theory, and we can't prove it. I suppose I'll have to tell Bradshaw, but he can wait for now. I'll call him later.'

'So, what do we do now?'

'Right now, we're going to eat our lunch. This afternoon, I think we should call in and see how young Spiderhair is doing, and then later maybe I'll call Bradshaw. It might be an idea to find Jasper again too. I have a feeling he's not telling us everything.'

CHAPTER TWENTY

It had been dark for an hour now, and there was a distinct chill in the air. The town was in that quiet phase after close of business, with just one or two shops still open. In an hour or two, things would liven up again, but for now all was quiet. As they walked through the town, Norman thought it seemed suitably appropriate for the sombre mood that had gripped them since they had left the hospital.

On the other side of the town centre, they turned down a narrow road. Twenty yards along, on the left, a collection of derelict factory buildings had been fenced off. Never one to miss an opportunity, the homeless Jasper had realised on his arrival in town that the site would provide enough old timber to feed a bonfire for months. He had a team of regulars who gathered every night to get warm, and this had provided him with another unexpected opportunity – this time, information gathering. He had soon discovered just how observant some of these homeless people were, and it hadn't taken long to find people willing to pay for information.

Hidden from view behind and between the buildings was a yard the size of a couple of tennis courts. If anyone passed this way at night and looked closely, they would notice an eerie red glow coming from this area. This was where Jasper had his nightly bonfire.

Norman stopped, grabbed the fence, and eased it apart, opening the gap used for access just wide enough for Darling to climb through. She then held the gap open for him to follow her.

'I wonder how hostile he's going to be tonight,' she said as they walked over to the buildings.

'I think he'll be okay until we tell him,' said Norman. 'That's when we'll find out how he really feels.'

They walked the rest of the way across the site and through to the bonfire in silence. As they emerged into the yard area, they could see a group of half a dozen or so sitting on upturned boxes close to the fire. One of the figures stood and watched as they approached. It was Jasper. They stopped just short of the small group and he stepped forward.

'You two just don't seem to be able to keep away, do you?'

Norman looked at the figures huddled together just behind Jasper, doing their best to absorb as much warmth as they could. 'D'you think we could talk?'

'It's a free country. You talk away, mate,' said Jasper, looking around confidently.

'I think it might be better if we talk in private,' said Norman quietly.

Something about his tone took the confident smile from Jasper's face, and he took a step towards them. 'Why? What's happened?'

Norman and Darling took a couple of steps back, and Jasper followed them. 'It's about Spiderhair,' said Norman. 'He's taken a turn for the worse. It turns out he's got a bleed on the brain. He's in a pretty bad way. It's touch and go.'

Even in the gloom, they could see Jasper's face had turned ashen. 'Oh shit, no!' He almost whispered the words. 'I told him he didn't need to do that.'

'The thing is, the hospital wants to notify his family, and we don't know where to find them,' continued Norman. 'I was hoping you might be able to tell them.'

'Family? I'm not even sure he had one. He certainly never mentioned them to me.'

'Would any of the others know?'

Jasper turned and shouted to the others. 'Anyone know Spider-hair's real name? Or where he came from?'

There were some mumbled replies and a lot of head shaking. None of them knew anything.

'The only one who might have known was that Ginger,' said Jasper, turning back to them, 'and you can't ask her now, can you? I told the kid he should have kept away from you two. I told him he should've kept quiet and let me do the talking.'

'Just now you said, "I told him he didn't need to do that". What did you mean?' asked Darling. 'Who didn't need to do what?'

Jasper looked at her and licked his lips. 'I think you must have heard wrong.'

'You know who did this to him, don't you?' demanded Darling, taking a step towards him.

'Don't talk rubbish,' he spat. 'Of course I don't.'

Darling was several inches shorter, but she was fearless, and she got right in his face. He took a step back, but she was relentless, and he suddenly found he had his back against a wall. Worse still, every head was turned their way, and all those people Jasper managed to keep down by bullying were watching him being bullied by a girl half his size.

'You're supposed to look out for these kids,' she hissed.

'It's your fault,' he argued. 'If you hadn't come around here asking questions and offering money, none of this would have happened'

'We've already held our hands up to that,' said Norman, angrily. 'But I seem to remember you knew what we were doing, and if you hadn't stormed off in a huff, you could have stopped him. Maybe we ought to tell the crew here what's happened to Spiderhair and how it might not have happened if only you hadn't stormed off.'

'It wasn't my f--'

Darling's eyes were blazing with a fierce intensity. 'It was as much your fault as it was ours,' she said, poking her finger in his chest to emphasis her point. 'But pointing the finger at each other isn't going to help anyone, is it? If you know who did this to him, you need to tell us so we can get something done about it!'

Such was Darling's ferocity, Jasper had involuntarily risen up onto his toes to try and escape, his arms crossed over his chest for protection.

Norman put a hand on Darling's arm, and she took a step back. 'Listen, Jasper,' he said, 'I've known Naomi for a couple of years now, but I have never seen her quite so upset before. I'm not one for advocating violence, but I'm quite sure she would feel a whole lot better if I let her beat the shit out of someone, and right now I think she'd be quite happy if it was you.'

Jasper was still pressed up against the wall, not daring to move. His eyes were as wide as saucers, and he seemed to have temporarily lost the power of speech.

Norman filled the silence for him. 'We know you're an informant for Jerry Shapiro, but we've spoken to him, and we know he has nothing to gain by attacking the kid. We also know someone is paying off the local police, and we know that's not Jerry. Are you with me so far?'

Jasper stared at Norman. He seemed to be too scared to look at Darling.

'Just nod if you can't speak,' Norman said. 'Are you with me so far?'

Jasper nodded frantically.

'That's very good, well done. Now, if you're with me so far, you should be able to see what we think this means. We think this means someone else is paying an informant, and now we think that informant is you. Are we right?'

He nodded his head again.

'So what's going on?' asked Norman. 'Is there some sort of turf war going on? Are you playing both sides at once? If you are, that's a very risky game.'

'It's not what you think,' spluttered Jasper.

Norman shook his head and smiled. 'No, it never is. It's amazing how many times I've heard that. If you're gonna persist with this bullshit, I may just have to let Naomi loose.'

'There's no need for that,' Jasper said hastily. 'Just get her away from me and I'll talk, but only to you.'

Norman sighed and smiled again. 'The thing is, me and Naomi, well, we're a team, so anything you have to say we both need to hear.'

Jasper was beginning to look like a rabbit caught in headlights.

'I tell you what I'll do. I'll ask Naomi to back off, okay?'

Jasper nodded furiously again. Norman looked at Darling and she took one small step back. 'There, how's that?' asked Norman, turning back to Jasper.

'That was hardly worth the effort, was it?'

'Well, don't say I didn't offer,' said Norman, as he began to turn away. 'Don't forget, she's highly trained and she really enjoys her job. And like I said, she's already seriously upset. I'll send flowers.'

'No, wait! When I say it's not like that, what I mean is there's no feud,' Jasper cried.

Norman raised an eyebrow as he turned back. 'So what's the deal?. Who else is paying you for information.'

'I'll get a good kicking if I tell you.'

'You'll get an even better one if you don't.'

'I only know him as "Driver". I don't know if that's his real name or if it's some sort of code name.'

'Code name?'

'Yeah. He's part of the drug squad. I keep my eyes open, especially down at the harbour, and I let him know if there's anything suspicious going on. He tells me which boats to watch out for, and I tell him when they come and go.'

'How do you contact him?'

'I wait at a call box at a set time and he calls me.'

'That's a bit hit and miss, isn't it? What if you're not there?'

'I'm always there,' Jasper said.

'I think that's more bullshit,' said Norman. 'You see, Spiderhair told us you go off on your own every day. I think you've got a bolt-hole somewhere here in town, a flat maybe, and I reckon that's where you go every day, and that's when you talk to this Driver guy. I bet you have a mobile phone there. Heck, you might even have one on you now.'

Jasper held up his hands. 'Look, all I know is he calls himself Driver, and he works for the drug squad. Why would I lie about that?'

All this time, Darling had been staring menacingly at Jasper, but now she spoke. 'What does he look like, this Driver?'

'I've hardly ever seen him since he first approached me.'

'Is he invisible?' she demanded.

'No, of course not.'

'So, if you've seen him, you should be able to tell us what he's like.'

'I didn't take that much notice. It's not as if I was trying to decide if I fancied him.'

Norman stepped forward, his fists clenched. 'D'you think this is some sort of joke?' he snarled. 'There's a woman lying dead on a slab in the local mortuary. There's a kid lying in a hospital bed who might die in the next couple of days. You told us you thought he was a good kid, so how about you stop pissing about and help us try to find out who did this? We think her death and Spiderhair's attack are connected, and probably the same guy did both. You claim to look out for these people, so how about you start doing it?'

Jasper swallowed, loud and hard. 'Well, when you put it like that, I suppose . . . But an undercover drug squad bloke wouldn't kill anyone, would he?'

'You know for sure he's in the drug squad?'

'Well, that's what he said.'

Norman sighed in exasperation.

'Look,' said Darling, 'we're not asking you to draw a bloody portrait. Just tell us what you can remember.'

For the first time, Jasper actually looked as if he was concentrating, and Norman thought that perhaps, at last, he was going to tell them the truth.

'He was tall,' he said.

'How tall?'

'Taller than me.'

Norman reckoned Jasper was about six feet one, and he started to get that old tingly feeling. He glanced at Darling. He could see she was getting it too. 'What else? Was he fat? Thin? What?'

'He had a big coat on, but I seem to remember thinking he was skinny, with sort of hunched shoulders. He had straggly, long hair and a sharp, beaky sort of nose. When I met him he was dressed in black. I remember now because he reminded me of a vulture.'

'Anything else?' asked Darling. 'Any distinguishing marks, like a tattoo?'

'I didn't see any, but then he had that big coat on, and his collar was turned up.'

———

Fifteen minutes later, Norman and Darling were walking back into town. 'So what do we think?' asked Darling. 'Is Jasper telling us the truth, or should we expect to find someone trying to run us down any minute?'

'That's a tough one,' said Norman. 'The description he gave us for this Driver guy is a pretty good match for the guy who ordered the pizza, so I think that much is true, but I'm not sure I buy the bit about him being drug squad.'

'Oh, come on, Norm. It fits perfectly if only you're prepared to accept Bradshaw is involved in Jenny's death. I think we should confront him and see what he has to say.'

'But we don't have any real proof! The guy might have told Jasper he was drug squad, but he could just as easily be working for Ben.'

'For God's sake, take those blinkers off,' Darling said. 'Just admit you got it wrong. Bradshaw's behind Jenny's death.'

'But what about the kid? Why would Bradshaw want him dead?'

'Because he was helping us learn too much. Don't forget, until he told us where he found Jenny's phone, we were getting nowhere fast. Maybe Bradshaw thought Spiderhair knew more than he actually did, so he had to be silenced.'

Norman sighed. What Naomi said could so easily be exactly what had happened. 'I'm still not convinced. I think we need more.'

'And how are we going to do that?'

'I dunno,' he said thoughtfully. 'Do you think you can remember how to get to Jerry's place?'

'Yes, sure.'

'Okay, let's make a deal. You drive us out to Jerry's now, and we'll speak to him again. If I can't find any answers there that will convince you I'm right, then we'll go and face Bradshaw.'

CHAPTER TWENTY-ONE

'I didn't expect to see you back here so soon,' said Jerry, smiling knowingly. 'Money's not so easy to turn down after all, is it?'

'Oh, we're not here for your money,' said Norman. 'We just have one or two more questions we think you might be able to help us with.'

Jerry's smile rapidly changed into a frown. 'What sort of questions?'

'Did you know you're not the only person paying Jasper for information?'

Jerry heaved a sigh of resignation. 'No, I didn't know, but I'm not really surprised. I suppose it goes with the territory. People who do what he's doing are unlikely to have much respect for loyalty, are they?'

Norman thought that sounded like the voice of a man who didn't much care any more. 'Don't you worry he's going to sell your secrets?'

'He doesn't know any secrets. Dennis deals with him, not me. Anyway, I don't really care what he does, to be honest. I just want to know who killed Jenny.'

'I'm afraid we still don't know that, but we have a lead you might be able to help us with. We think the other guy Jasper deals with is a drug squad officer.'

Jerry leaned forward. 'You think the drug squad had her killed? But why?'

'No, no, of course not,' said Norman hastily. 'But we think Jenny's death is linked with the local drug scene, and we think if we can find this guy, he may know something that would help us.'

'The local drug scene? What would her death have to do with that?'

'It's a theory,' said Norman. 'We know drugs come in through the harbour here, and we think it's possible the people responsible would like to reach the biggest market of all, which is London. So it figures they could be the people who were making all the threats about Jenny before.'

Jerry's eyes widened. 'You think bringing her here led to her death? God, that would mean it was my fault, wouldn't it?'

'Let's not jump to any conclusions,' said Norman. 'Like I said, it's just an idea. If I can find this guy, maybe he can tell me if it's worth pursuing. I don't suppose you have any idea where I might find him?'

'D'you really think drug squad officers are the sort of people I usually socialise with?'

'No, but I figure it might help to know your enemy and know his movements, if you get my drift.'

'That would be something my brother might know, but I'm afraid I can't help you with it. I suppose I can always ask him.'

'You're in contact with him? I thought you were leaving all that behind!'

'Yes, well, there doesn't seem much point now, does there?' Jerry said sadly. 'I'm better off with my family than on my own.'

'What's his take on all this?' asked Darling.

'He thinks it's someone trying to frighten us off. He's told me to stay down here until I find out who's behind it, but if you can tell me something about this guy, maybe Ben can fill in some blanks.'

'Apparently he goes by the name of Driver,' said Darling.

Jerry's head snapped around to face her. 'Driver?'

'Yeah. D'you know him?'

'Err, no. It just seems a weird sort of name, that's all.'

Norman was watching Jerry closely. 'We don't know if that's his surname, nickname, or if it's some sort of code name.'

'Any idea what he looks like?' asked Jerry.

'Tall, skinny, a bit stooped,' said Darling. 'Likes to wear a big coat that makes him look like a vulture.'

'Sounds like he's a pretty distinctive-looking guy. I'm sure Ben will remember him if he's come across him before.'

'You're sure you don't know him?' asked Norman, 'Only you seemed to recognise that name.'

Jerry laughed. 'No, not at all. I just thought it was a bit of a weird name. Like I said, Ben might know more.'

'Okay,' said Norman, doubtfully. 'It might well come to nothing, but every lead's worth following up, you know?'

'Yes, fine. Leave it with me. Leave me your number and I'll let you know what he says. Now if you don't mind, I have guests.'

'Oh, sorry,' said Norman. 'You should have said. We'll get out of your hair.'

————

'D'you think he really had people there?' asked Darling, when they were in the car, heading back to town.

'Well, he didn't let us past the front door, so maybe.'

'He knows who we're talking about, doesn't he? Did you see his face when I mentioned the name?'

'Yeah, he knows alright, but if he doesn't want to tell us who it is, it's not really much help, is it?'

'You realise you're going to have to keep your end of the bargain now, don't you?' said Darling. 'He didn't say anything that made me change my mind about Bradshaw. In fact, if he knows this Driver, the drug squad guy, that more or less wraps it up for me.'

'I wish I was as certain as you,' said Norman. 'Something's not right about this, but I can't see what it is.'

'It's those Bradshaw blinkers you're wearing. We'll go and confront him in the morning, and you'll see I'm right.'

'Okay, I suppose it was my idea, and we did make a deal. But we're not going tomorrow. Tomorrow is Sunday, and we're going to have a rest day. We'll drive up there on Monday morning after breakfast.'

'And you promise you won't tell him we're coming?'

'I promise,' said Norman.

CHAPTER TWENTY-TWO

As they drove out of town on Monday morning, they passed a large sign that said 'Thank you for visiting Redville-on-Sea'. Darling decided this would be as good a time as any to broach the subject Norman seemed to be struggling to come to terms with. 'I do understand why you have a problem accepting Bradshaw could be behind this.'

'You do?'

'Of course. You've known him for a long time, he has a reputation for being honest, and he's known to take good care of his staff.'

'He was always as straight as an arrow when I worked with him,' said Norman. 'I just find it hard to accept he would have used Jenny like that.'

'He was tipped for the top. Wasn't that what you said about him?'

'Yeah, that's right, he was destined for great things.'

'So what happened?' asked Darling.

'How d'you mean?'

'Well, what he's doing now isn't exactly sitting at the top table, is it?'

'I haven't seen the guy since he shot past me up that greasy pole years ago, but this thing he heads is a new project. It's his baby.'

'You really think digging up cold cases and taking on the stuff no one else cares about is en route to the top?'

'All that ladder-climbing shit never interested me, so, if I'm honest, I can't say I've given it much thought.'

Darling smiled knowingly. 'I guessed as much, so I got my laptop out last night and did some bedtime reading.'

Norman gave her a sideways look. 'And?'

'Well, I can't say for sure, but from what I can see, this "project" isn't such a big deal unless your name's Bradshaw and you're trying to impress people who aren't in the know.'

Norman raised an eyebrow. 'What's that supposed to mean?'

'Well, he's told you it's some serious, big-deal job, right? But the reality is it's only <u>his</u> baby because no one else wanted it, and he had no other choice but to take it.'

'You mean it's a sideways promotion?'

'It's actually a "sideways into a backwater" promotion. As far as Bradshaw's career is concerned, the route to the top has been well and truly closed.'

Norman let out a whistle. 'He must have messed up big time.'

'That's what I thought, so I dug around to see what I could find, and guess what?'

Norman looked across at her again, and she gave him a triumphant grin in return.

'You know what I'm going to say, don't you?' she said.

Norman shook his head in disbelief. 'Oh crap! Don't tell me . . .'

'D'you think you might put the blinkers away now?'

CHAPTER TWENTY-THREE

'Come in,' called a voice from the other side of the door. Norman leaned on the handle, pushed the door open, and walked through, Darling hot on his heels. From behind his desk, Bradshaw's face was a picture of surprise. 'Norm! You should have called,' he said, as he began to rise from his seat.

'No, it's okay, don't bother to get up,' said Norman. 'This shouldn't take long.'

'You didn't need to come all the way up here, I would have met you halfway.' Bradshaw nodded to Darling. 'Naomi.'

'I bet you would have preferred that,' said Norman, 'but we've more or less wrapped up this case now.'

'You have?'

'Like I said, more or less. There are one or two things we're not quite clear about, but we thought you could help us with those.'

Bradshaw looked puzzled. 'Me? How can I help?'

'When we spoke the other day, you told us there wasn't anything else we needed to know. You said you had told us everything.'

'Yes, that's right.'

'But it's not right, is it? You forget to mention what was probably the most important thing of all.'

Bradshaw looked vacant.

'Don't try to stall us with that dumb "I don't know what you mean" crap. We know about you and the Shapiro trial.'

'Ah, yes, that,' said Bradshaw. 'I suppose I probably should have mentioned it.'

'You "should have mentioned it"?' echoed Norman. 'You denied being involved! You even said you never worked for the drug squad.'

'I didn't think it was relevant.'

'Of course it's relevant, that's why you lied about it! Losing that case put an end to all your promotion hopes, didn't it?'

Bradshaw shook his head vigorously. 'It wasn't like that.'

'So why don't you tell us what it was like? Because from where we're standing, you've got one hell of a motive for making sure Jenny died!'

Bradshaw looked shocked. 'Who the hell do you think you are? You can't come barging in here accusing me of murder!'

'So what should we accuse you of?' asked Darling.

Now Bradshaw's eyes were blazing, and he pointed an angry finger at her. 'This is outrageous! I've never heard such twaddle in all my life. Jenny was a family friend. I've known her father for many years. When she went off the rails, he asked me if I could find out what had happened to her.'

Never taking her eyes from his, Darling stepped slowly up to his desk, placed her hands on the edge, leaned towards him, and then spoke very slowly and clearly. 'If you know her father so well, you'll know he's been in a nursing home since her mother died a couple of years ago. His Alzheimer's is bad enough he had stopped recognising his own daughter, so I very much doubt he would have known who you were, and he certainly wouldn't have been asking for your help to keep track of her.'

Bradshaw's mouth opened and closed a couple of times.

'You like chess, don't you, Bradshaw?' said Norman. 'I think you'll find that's what they call "check".'

'What I meant was, the nursing home asked me on his behalf,' said Bradshaw, unconvincingly.

Norman heaved a heavy sigh, pulled a chair across in front of Bradshaw's desk, and sat down. 'Even you don't believe that,' he said wearily, 'and frankly I'm getting tired of all this bullshit. You know me well enough to know I'm not going to let this go , so do us all a favour, save us some time, and tell us what's really been going on.'

'I thought you had it all worked out,' said Bradshaw after a moment.

'I think we have,' said Norman, 'but I'd like to hear it from you. Straight from the horse's mouth, you know?'

'If you think I killed her, you're barking up the wrong tree. I had nothing to do with it.'

'I thought you were going to stop feeding us bullshit.'

'Do you want to hear me out or not?' snapped Bradshaw.

'I've got a better idea,' said Norman. 'Why don't I tell you what we think happened? At least that way we can avoid all the crap you're going to send our way.'

Darling had found herself a chair and pulled it over and settled alongside Norman.

'Okay, this is our theory,' began Norman. 'When Jenny tore your Shapiro case to shreds and got it kicked out of court, you were left up the proverbial creek. This had been the big case that was going to propel you even further up that greasy pole, maybe even all the way to the top, but now your whole career was going be put in limbo. This was the end of the line, unless you could somehow get the better of the Shapiros. So you approached Jenny and you tried to persuade her to work for you. You knew she and Jerry had a thing going, so you tried to get her to work against him, but she wouldn't play ball.'

'That's not how it was--' said Bradshaw, but Norman cut him short with a wave of his hand.

'You don't get to speak until I finish,' he said. 'Then you can try and spin your way out of it. Until then, you can just listen. I wouldn't be at all surprised if you had something to do with Jenny's career going pear-shaped at that point, but it didn't really matter because she had already decided to get out and shack up with Jerry. Then you tried to get her onboard again, and she told you what you could do. She even told Jerry you had approached her. Not long after that, she started getting threats.'

Bradshaw looked surprised. 'Threats? I didn't know anything about any threats.'

'I think you do,' said Darling.

'We can worry about the details later,' said Norman. 'You haven't denied anything else I've mentioned, so I guess that means we're more or less right so far.'

'What you've presented is a very interesting theory,' said Bradshaw, 'but that's all it is. You can't possibly have any proof, because I know for a fact that not one word of it is true.'

'There was a point where I was willing to believe you weren't involved,' admitted Norman. 'It was misplaced loyalty on my part, of course. But unluckily for you, I brought Naomi along. I told you she was a good foil for me, didn't I? It was Naomi who found out about Jenny's parents.'

Bradshaw looked daggers at Darling, but she simply stared impassively back at him.

'And she had the sense to check out the Shapiro trial. Up until then, I had no idea you'd ever worked on the drug squad. The worst thing was, you had lied to me about it, and that's what finally convinced me I was wrong and she was right.'

Bradshaw stared at Norman. 'Nearly everyone who wants to get anywhere works there at some stage,' he said. 'You have to know how it all works when you get to the top.'

'Yeah, but you didn't just work there – you took the lead in a major case,' said Norman. 'Anyway, once Naomi found that link, it all seemed to fit, and I understood where that guy Driver came into it.'

Bradshaw's eyes darted between the two of them. 'Driver? What the hell are you talking about?'

'Tall, skinny guy, big black coat, looks like a vulture.'

Bradshaw stared at Norman.

'Driver is the guy you have on the inside of the Shapiro organisation,' Norman said. 'I dunno how long he's been undercover in there, but he must be pretty good. Apparently he's risen high enough to become Ben Shapiro's enforcer.'

'I don't know what you're talking about. How could I have someone undercover? I left the drug squad years ago.'

'I'm sure he's not your agent now, but you put him in there, didn't you? And having got him in there, it's quite possible you're still able to contact him.'

Bradshaw slammed his fist on his desk. 'I've had enough of this. It's preposterous! I did not send an undercover officer to infiltrate the Shapiros, and even if I had, do you seriously think I would still be able to contact him? Are you mad?'

'Maybe I am,' said Norman. 'But we have a witness who saw a guy matching Driver's description chase Jenny in front of a car. The car deliberately ran her down, and then Driver jumped in the car and they sped off, leaving her lying at the side of the road with a broken leg. A couple of minutes later, they came back, stuffed her in the car, and then drove off with her.'

Bradshaw shrugged. 'I still don't see how you think you can link any of this to me. Jenny was a family friend.'

'So you keep saying,' said Norman. 'But let's not forget she was also the person who screwed up your career, wasn't she?'

Bradshaw stared silently at Norman, his face a picture of malevolence.

'Anyhow,' continued Norman, 'it gets worse for your friend, Driver. When Jenny's body was found, there was a half-eaten pizza on a table nearby. For whatever reason, the local police didn't think this was worth checking out, but we did. It turns out the pizza was bought from a shop in town, by a guy who, once again, matched Driver's description.

'And I have to say, he is one mean, nasty, piece of work. We believe he stuck a needle in Jenny's arm, injected enough heroin to kill an elephant, and then sat there eating pizza while he watched her die.'

'That's appalling,' said Bradshaw. 'But you have to believe me when I say I have nothing to do with this man, and I'm sure he is not an undercover officer. There never was anyone in that position, and as far as I know, there still isn't.'

'He's put a kid in hospital too. The poor kid showed us where he found Jenny's phone, and the next thing he knows, he's being run down by a car. Quite a coincidence, don't you think? That kid is in a really bad way, and if he dies, that'll be murder number two for Mr Driver. It seems the car is his weapon of choice. I guess that's why he got the name, huh?'

Bradshaw sighed wearily, and his shoulders slumped. 'It's a wonderfully imaginative theory, but I'm afraid you've got so many details wrong you've ended up rather wide of the mark.'

'So why don't you tell us where we've gone wrong?' Norman asked.

'Driver is, as you say, Ben Shapiro's enforcer, but he's not an undercover drug squad officer, nor is he any sort of asset. He's a bit of a sadist who's there to do the Shapiro's dirty work.'

Norman glanced at Darling. 'You're not convincing me,' she said.

'I don't have to convince you. Don't forget who's in charge around here.'

'Being in charge doesn't give you carte blanche.'

Bradshaw looked suitably affronted, but he didn't speak.

'Why would Ben Shapiro tell Driver to kill Jenny?' asked Norman.

'Why do you think he sent out the threats when she first went to live with Jerry? He never wanted her anywhere near their business back then, and he certainly didn't want her taking his brother away now.'

Norman stared at Bradshaw, and his face broke into a low steady grin.

'What?' asked Bradshaw, 'What's that stupid face for?'

'Well, I'm just wondering how you know all this about Ben and Jerry.'

'I told you before, we thought there was some sort of feud.'

'Yeah, but you also said surveillance was really difficult, and you didn't know what the feud was about. Now it seems you do know, so who's your source?'

'I don't have a "source". It didn't take a lot of working out, did it?' snapped Bradshaw.

'It certainly didn't if someone's reporting back to you.'

'Or of it was your idea in the first place,' suggested Darling.

Bradshaw glared at Darling. 'You really don't like me, do you?'

'Is it that obvious?'

'Patently.'

'Good, I'd hate you to be in any doubt.'

'I'm sorry, Norm,' said Bradshaw, 'but if you intend to make Ms

Darling a permanent member of your team, I don't think I will be using your services again.'

'I don't remember suggesting I wanted to offer my services again,' said Norman.

Bradshaw raised his eyebrows.

'Sorry,' continued Norman, 'but there are too many unanswered questions here for me to be able to trust you the way I once did.'

'What? You'd give up this opportunity just because this girl—'

'Let me stop you right there,' said Norman. 'It has nothing to do with "this girl". It's all to do with you. When we were called in to do this job, we were supposed to see it as dead simple and straightforward. We were supposed to accept it was a suicide, even though you already knew it wasn't. You even had a backup scenario in case we didn't accept the suicide idea. In that scenario, we would find out Ben and Jerry had fallen out, and as a result Ben had killed Jenny – or got this guy called Driver – to kill her. That should have been it: case closed, and no blame attached to you. Am I right?'

'But that is what you've found, isn't it? It seems to be what you've just told me!'

'But it's not that, is it?' said Norman. 'You should have thought twice about paying off Casey. He was so unconvincing, he made us suspicious right from the start.'

'Casey? Who's Casey?'

'Casey's the guy who handled the report when Jenny was found. It's funny you can't remember him. He remembers you, and he remembers the phone call you made to him.'

Darling's mouth dropped open, and she turned to Norman.

'I'm sorry I didn't tell you earlier,' he said, 'but you weren't the only one who did some research last night. He was on the late shift, so I went and spoke to him.'

He turned back to Bradshaw. 'That was another thing you forgot to mention. You must have known Jenny was dead within hours of it happening. Casey says you called him that same night.'

'I had an urgent alert out for anyone matching her description,' admitted Bradshaw. 'Of course I knew.'

'I was a police officer for a long, long time,' said Norman. 'I know how those alerts work, and I know it's not often they work that bloody fast. But, of course, there is another way you could have been alerted.'

'You can check. You'll see it was the alert that notified me,' shouted Bradshaw.

'You can bet we'll check, and it might even prove you're right, but at the very least, you've messed up big time, and Jenny got murdered as a result. What I can't decide is if it was down to bad luck, bad decisions, or did you actually arrange for her to be killed?'

'For God's sake! Why on earth would I do that?' The phone began to ring on Bradshaw's desk. He glanced at it, and then at Norman.

'Go ahead and answer it,' said Norman. 'We can wait.'

Bradshaw picked up the phone and listened. Norman watched as a smile briefly flirted with the corners of his mouth, but it was dismissed before it could spread any further. He listened for a further minute or so before he spoke. 'Can you bring the report in and the photographs? Thank you.'

He put the phone down and looked up at Norman. 'Tell me, when you had your little chat with Jerry Shapiro, did you suggest Ben might have been behind Jenny's death?'

Now it was Norman's turn to be uncomfortable. 'We asked him if he knew anyone called Driver.'

'And did he admit to knowing him?'

'No, but we got the impression he was lying about that.'

There was a knock on the door. Bradshaw walked across to the door, opened it, reached out, mumbled a few words, closed the door, and then retreated back into the room. He opened the folder he was carrying as he walked to his desk. He smiled at them as he sat down.

'Well, now, it seems detectives Norman and Darling might not be quite as clever as they think they are.'

He placed some photos on the table, quickly sorted through them, picked out three, and then placed them carefully on the desk in front of them.

'Take look at these photographs,' he said. 'They were taken about an hour ago. You might want to pat yourselves on the back, as this seems to be a direct result of your last conversation with Jerry Shapiro.'

They leaned forward to look at the photos. As they did, Bradshaw pointed to the first. 'This is Ben Shapiro. As you can see, he's taken a shotgun blast to the chest at close range. He's dead, of course.'

He pointed to the second photograph. 'You can probably guess who this one is. As you said, he looks rather like a vulture. This is the man known as Driver. He's nothing to do with the drug squad, but he is Ben Shapiro's right-hand man. He, too, has been gunned down in the same manner.'

'You know the man in the third photo, of course, as you've met him.'

Norman had been completely wrong-footed by the arrival of the photographs and was having trouble processing what was in front of him, but now he could feel the blood draining from his face as he suddenly realised what Bradshaw was showing them. 'Jerry,' he said, quietly.

He glanced at Darling. She had both hands to her mouth, her face ashen and eyes wide. He reached a hand out to her and squeezed her arm.

'That's right, Norm. Very good,' Bradshaw purred sarcastically. 'I can't imagine how it happened, but it seems Jerry somehow got it into his head that Ben and Driver were responsible for Jenny's death, so this morning he took his revenge with a shotgun. As you can see, he's in handcuffs, and he has been charged with two counts of murder.'

Norman looked up at Bradshaw. 'But we had no way of knowing he would do this,' he said, his voice a hoarse whisper.

'Aren't you going to blame me for this as well, Ms Darling?' asked Bradshaw gleefully. 'Or perhaps you're not quite so confident about your case now?'

Darling was shaking her head in disbelief, tears welling in her eyes.

'Oh, don't look so upset. You've actually done a wonderful job between you. I think you should be congratulated. The world will be a much better place without someone like Ben Shapiro around. We've been trying to stop him for years, and now you two have done it in a matter of days. And no one can save him this time, can they?'

Norman was still too stunned to say anything, and Darling was bereft.

'Perhaps you two aren't cut out for this tough stuff,' said Bradshaw. 'I suppose haranguing an innocent man like me is far easier to stomach.'

'Yeah, about that,' began Norman.

'There isn't a shred of evidence to prove any of this is down to me, is there?' said Bradshaw. 'But it's possible two rogue detectives incited a man to take a shotgun and commit two murders.'

'Now, just a minute,' said Norman. 'You can't be serious.'

'Can't I? Give me one good reason why I shouldn't.'

CHAPTER TWENTY-FOUR

F ive minutes earlier, a newish Range Rover had turned into the car
park and screeched to a halt. The driver switched off the engine
and turned to his passenger. 'Right,' said Slater. 'You're quite sure you
want to do this? I know he's your boss, but this whole case has been a
bloody wild goose chase right from the start. I don't mind following
leads, but we've been up and down the north of England like a pair of
bloody yo-yos looking for people who died years ago.'

'I'm with you,' agreed Watson. 'It's been a complete waste of time.'

'We might as well have been on holiday for all the good we've
done.'

'I'm as annoyed as you, honestly.'

'Right. Come on, then,' said Slater. 'Let's see what he has to say for
himself.'

He jumped from the car and stormed angrily across the car park,
Watson doing her best to keep up with him. 'Perhaps there's been a
mistake,' she said, hopefully.

'The mistake has been Bradshaw's if he thinks he can send us off to
bugger about like that all the time. I came here to be a detective, not a
bloody errand boy.'

Watson thought there wasn't much point in arguing with him. He'd been getting more and more annoyed as the case had progressed, and some of the language he had used on the journey home had reminded her of her army days.

Secretly, she thought falling out with his girlfriend had upset him more than he let on. He had told her he had known it was coming and that he didn't really care, but she hadn't been convinced. And there must be some sort of hangover from the Diana Randall case, whatever the psychologist might have said.

She could understand why he was annoyed. After all, no one likes wasting their time, but his anger seemed to be disproportionate, and as they entered the building, she found herself hoping he wasn't going to do anything stupid.

They had reached the corridor that led to Bradshaw's office now. Normally they would call in to see his secretary to make sure he was free, but today Slater wasn't in the mood for protocol. He wanted answers.

'Shouldn't we check to make sure he's free?' asked Watson.

'He'll just stall for time if he knows we're here,' said Slater. They had reached Bradshaw's door now, and as Slater reached for the handle with one hand, he knocked with the other and walked inside.

He stopped so abruptly that Watson almost walked into him. She edged to one side and peered over his shoulder. A man and woman were sitting on two chairs in front of Bradshaw's desk. They were staring at some photos. The man had looked around and was staring at them, his mouth wide open in a perfectly round 'O' of surprise. Watson knew the face, but for a moment, she was so surprised she couldn't think of his name.

Slater had no such problem. 'Norm? What are you doing here?'

Now the woman looked around too. 'You too, Naomi? What is this?'

'How dare you come bursting into my office like this,' roared Bradshaw. 'Have you no manners? My secretary should have told you--'

'Your secretary doesn't even know we're here,' said Slater, 'so don't blame her. We've come straight here because we want some answers.'

'If you want answers, you'll have to come back later. You can see I'm busy. Now get out.'

Slater was at Bradshaw's desk now. 'We've just wasted over a week running around like a pair of idiots. Tell me why, and I'll leave.'

'I don't know what you're talking about,' said Bradshaw.

'Sure you do,' said Slater. 'That wasn't a case we were on, it was more like a game of hide and bloody seek but with no one to find. You must have known that!'

'It was an important case that needed--' began Bradshaw.

'We needed to get you out of the way for a few days,' said Norman. 'I said it was a stupid idea and we shoulda told you, but he insisted it would be okay and it would be better if you didn't know.'

'Didn't know what?'

'Inspector Slater, I suggest you take Sergeant Brearley with you and step outside – now,' warned Bradshaw.

'What's been going on, Norm?' asked Slater, ignoring his boss, 'Why did you need me out of the way?'

Darling was in tears, obviously deeply upset by something, and Watson automatically stepped forward to console her

'I can give you the long story later,' began Norman.

'You will tell him nothing,' snapped Bradshaw. 'I'll tell him myself when he returns later, as instructed.'

Slater looked at Bradshaw with an expression bordering on contempt. He could feel words he would regret forming in his mouth, but he managed to stop himself before they escaped. Instead, he focused his attention on Norman. 'Go on, Norm, let's hear it.'

'I'm not quite sure how best to tell you this. I'm sorry, Dave, but Jenny's dead.'

Slater tried to speak, but it was as if he had been punched hard in the guts. All the wind seemed to have been driven from his lungs.

'She got herself involved with some drug dealers and ended up being murdered.'

Slater managed to take a breath. 'Was this the Shapiros?' he asked.

'You knew?' asked a shocked Norman.

'Yeah, she told me.'

'You never said.'

'We decided it was better if no one knew. She knew I felt like a fool for being played like that. I think she wanted to spare me the embarrassment. But how did it happen? Why? Who did it?'

'Well, that's what me and Naomi have been trying to find out,' said Norman. 'I feel terrible going behind your back, but we thought it was for the best, what with you being so closely involved with her.'

'Now just a minute,' said Bradshaw. 'I'm supposed to be in charge here.'

Watson had been studying the photographs on the table, and now she spoke. 'Isn't that the Shapiros in that photo?'

'Yeah,' said Norman.

'And isn't that other guy called Driver? He's your man on the inside, isn't he, sir?' she asked.

Norman and Slater turned to Watson. 'Can you say that again?' asked Norman, jumping to his feet.

Watson pointed at the middle photo. 'That man. He's known as Driver. He's the drug squad's paid informer in the Shapiro organisation. Mr Bradshaw recruited him years ago.'

All eyes were suddenly on Bradshaw. His face had gone a strange colour, and he seemed to have lost his tongue. Darling was struggling to free herself from Watson's arms.

'You bastard,' she hissed at Bradshaw. 'You were pulling the strings behind this all the time, weren't you? I bet you told him to suggest Ben start threatening Jenny, didn't you?'

'I don't know what you're talking about,' said Bradshaw. 'It's all fantasy. You can't prove any of it. And what does it matter? The world's a better place without the likes of the Shapiros on the streets.'

'What about Jenny?' snarled Norman. 'What about the poor kid lying in a coma?'

'That's very unfortunate,' conceded Bradshaw, 'but when these people start to tear each other apart, there are always innocent victims.'

'That's three murders,' said Norman, 'and possibly a fourth if the kid doesn't recover, and you think that's okay? How do you sleep at night?'

'Oh, grow up, Norman,' sneered Bradshaw. 'The reason these

people flourish is because of people like you who pussyfoot around making sure no one gets hurt.'

'You really are behind all of this, aren't you?'

Bradshaw folded his arms and stared at Norman. 'Rubbish,' he said. 'You can't prove it, and you know it.'

Slater had been digging in his pockets. He threw his warrant card at Bradshaw.

'What this?' asked Bradshaw.

'I'm out of here,' said Slater, 'and I won't be coming back.'

'I order you to stay right where you are.'

'If I stay here much longer, there's going to be another murder,' said Slater, 'only I like to think I'm better than that.' He turned on his heel and marched from the office.

'Slater, come back here,' called Bradshaw.

Watson ran after Slater. 'Sir,' she called. 'Sir, wait.'

He was away down the corridor, and she couldn't tell if he heard her or not, but she wasn't letting him get away that easily, and she rushed after him. It was as he pushed his way through the doors into the car park that she caught up with him. 'Sir, wait, please.'

He stopped, but didn't turn around, so she ran to stand in front of him.

'You can't leave like this!'

Slater sighed and studied his feet for a moment. When he looked up, she could see the tears in his eyes.

'D'you know,' he said, 'ever since I came to work here, that man has made a point of asking me how Jenny is, what she's up to, what she talks about. I used to think he was passing on what I said on to her parents, but when she told me about the Shapiros, Jenny also told me about her parents. He wasn't reporting back to them. He was just keeping tabs on her. That's one of the reasons why I didn't tell anyone why she left. I figured if Bradshaw didn't know, she might have a chance to get away without him finding out. I didn't know he had a guy on the inside there.'

'Do you think he really could have arranged her death?' asked Watson.

'I dunno, Sam. Norm seems to think so, and he's not often wrong.'

'What are you going to do?'

'I can't stay here. If I don't kill the man, I certainly won't ever respect him or trust him. You must be able to see that.'

'Yes, of course I can,' she said. 'It's just . . . I don't know, I suppose I'm just being selfish, but I've really enjoyed working with you. I don't want it to stop.'

'If it's any consolation, I think you're the best, I really do, but I can't stay here, even for you.'

'I don't know what I'm going to do,' she said, a small tear beginning to glisten in the corner of one eye.

'You're going to stay here and keep working,' he said. 'You've worked bloody hard to get where you are, and you'll be a DI before much longer. You don't want to throw all that away, do you?'

'I suppose not.'

He reached a hand to her face and gently wiped the tear away with his thumb. He smiled encouragingly. 'You look after yourself, and make sure you keep that bionic knee well oiled, d'you hear me.'

She nodded.

'I'd better go before I change my mind and go back in there,' he said.

'Can I do one thing before you go?'

'Sure,' he said.

She stepped forward and kissed him, her lips a gentle, warm, softness on his. 'It wouldn't have been right and proper for me to kiss my boss,' she said as she stepped back, 'but now, if you're not going to be my boss, well . . .'

She smiled a slightly shy smile, then turned and walked back through the doors, stopping to look through the window and offer a quick wave before she disappeared from view.

Slater licked his lips, as if he needed to make sure that had really happened, and then headed for his car.

CHAPTER TWENTY-FIVE

F ive minutes later Norman and Darling emerged from the building and crossed the car park. As Darling started her car, Norman's mobile phone started to ring. 'Yeah, Norman,' he called wearily into the phone.

'It's Steve Casey here. Remember me?'

'Yeah, of course I remember,' said Norman, 'though I have to say you're not exactly a fond memory. What do you want?'

'It's the kid in hospital. You've been to visit him a couple of times, so I thought you'd want to know.'

'Want to know what? Has he come round?'

'I'm afraid not. It's gone the other way.'

'You mean he's got worse?'

'No, I mean he's dead.'

Norman couldn't quite believe his ears. 'What?'

'I just got a call from the hospital. They couldn't save him, he died a couple of hours ago.'

Norman had been trying hard to keep the alarm out of his voice, but now he realised Darling had picked up on it, and the car hadn't moved an inch.

'What is it?' she asked.

'I'll call you back in a few minutes,' Norman told Casey and ended the call.

'Norm, what is it?' she asked again.

He tossed his phone onto the floor and turned to face her. 'It's Spiderhair,' he said. 'They couldn't save him. The poor kid died a couple of hours ago.'

At first her face seemed to freeze in a horrible mask of shock, but then the tears came, and as they did they seemed to wash all expression away. Norman reached across and held her to him while she sobbed her heart out.

'I'm so sorry,' he said, when she had finally calmed down. 'You really liked him, didn't you?'

'He was a nice kid,' she sobbed. 'Why did anyone need to hurt him?'

'I know,' said Norman, softly. 'He didn't deserve any of this.'

'He would have been all on his own when he died,' she wailed. 'Someone should have been there for him. I should have been there!'

'We didn't know he was going to die,' said Norman.

'I still should have been there,' she said. 'No one should die like that with nobody to care. I want to go back. I want to try and find his family, or at least make sure he gets a proper funeral.'

'We'll go back down tomorrow--'

'No, I want to go right now!' she said.

'Okay, okay,' he said. 'But let me drive. You're way too upset.'

'I'm fine.'

'You are not. I'll only come with you if you let me drive.'

'That bloody Bradshaw has to pay for this,' she said. 'He can't get away with it.'

'Yeah, but he didn't actually kill anyone, did he?' said Norman. 'It was Driver that ran the kid down, and he's dead. We can't prove anything.'

'There must be something we can get him for,' said Darling. 'We've got to get him, Norm.'

'We'll never prove he killed anyone, and I doubt we can prove he set this all up. He's not denying he knows Driver, and Driver is the only one who knew the truth. C'mon, let's change places and I'll drive.'

Reluctantly Darling eased her door open and climbed from the car.

'Can I use your phone?' she asked, as she settled in the passenger seat.

'Help yourself, it's on the floor down there somewhere.'

She found the phone and hit redial. 'Casey? It's Naomi Darling.'

'Oh, I was going to call you.'

'You were? What for?'

'I've been thinking about that kid. I'm partly responsible for his death, and I want to do the right thing.'

'I'm sorry?'

'It's my fault your friend's death was swept under the carpet, and it's my fault this kid's dead. I never meant things to go that far.'

'What exactly do you mean, when you say "it's your fault"?'

'It was just meant to be a bit of easy money, you know? Look the other way, and say what I was told to say. I admit I'm lazy, and I've taken the odd backhander before, but I didn't know anyone was going to get hurt.'

'So what are you going to do?'

'I'd like to make a statement.'

'What sort of statement?'

There was a sigh. 'I was in the middle. I passed messages from Bradshaw to Driver. I could have stopped it. If I had refused to pass the messages on, your friends might still be alive.'

'You're serious?'

'I am.'

'We're on the way there now.'

'I'm on lates,' said Casey. 'Call me when you get here and I'll come and meet you.'

Darling ended the call and turned to Norman. 'Casey wants to make a statement about Bradshaw!'

'Yeah? Is he for real?'

'He sounds it. He says he was passing information from Bradshaw to Driver. It might not prove murder, but it should be enough to finish his bloody career.'

'Well, I guess even a small victory would be better than none at all,' said Norman, as he put the car into gear.

In the middle of the car park he could see Slater was sitting in his car, talking on his mobile phone, so he eased alongside and wound down his window. He watched as Slater ended his phone call, then his window glided smoothly down.

'Are you okay?' asked Norman.

'Yeah, I guess so. Jenny didn't deserve that, you know?'

'Yeah, tell me about it. That bastard organised it, and he thinks he's got away with it.'

'Bradshaw's a slippery sod,' said Slater. 'He will have covered his tracks. He knows you can't prove he was involved, doesn't he? The only guy who could have proved it was Driver, and he's dead.'

Norman grinned. 'Yeah, that's what we thought, but we just got a call from Bradshaw's go-between down on the coast. It seems this guy has a conscience. He's offered to make a confession. D'you wanna come?'

'Yeah, well, good luck with that,' said Slater, starting his car, 'and thanks for the offer, but right now I feel I've had enough of this stuff to last a lifetime.'

'Are you going home?'

Slater pursed his lips. 'I dunno.' He wiggled the phone in his hand. 'I was going to, but now I'm thinking I might take a detour on the way.'

'Anywhere nice?'

'You might call it the promised land.' Slater winked, put his car into gear, and eased away. Norman stared after him.

'Where did he say he was going?' asked Darling.

'I think he said, "the promised land".'

'What does that mean?'

'I have no idea.'

<<<<>>>>

BOOKS BY P.F. FORD

ABOUT THE AUTHOR

A late starter to writing after a life of failures, P.F. (Peter) Ford spent most of his life being told he should forget his dreams, and that he would never make anything of himself without a "proper" job.

But then a few years ago, having been unhappy for over 50 years of his life, Peter decided he had no intention of carrying on that way. Fast forward a few years and you find a man transformed by a partner (now wife) who believed dreamers should be encouraged and not denied.

Now, happily settled in Wales, Peter is blissfully happy sharing his life with wife Mary and their four rescue dogs, and living his dream writing fiction (and still without a "proper" job).

learn more here:
www.pfford.co.uk

Printed in Great Britain
by Amazon

43625579R00096